THE FROZEN TRAIL

ADVANCE PRAISE

The Frozen Trail

The Willie Handcart Company endured unimaginable sorrow and tragedy, vividly shown in the novel *The Frozen Trail*. Lisa Dayley brings the story to life and draws you in. You'll feel how truly cold, hungry and desperate the pioneers were. It also shows how resilient they were, and, in particular, Emma Girdlestone who sacrificed everything she had for her new religion.

~Jon Schmidt,
pianist and recording artist

It is easy to feel as if you are there on the trek with Emma Girdlestone. Kudos to Dayley for a well-written book.

~Howard Carlos Smith,
Keeper of the Prophet's Sword

A thrill to read, Lisa Dayley crafts a genuine pioneer story with just the right mix of fact and fiction. You'll find this book hard to put down.

~Jay Lenkersdorfer,
newpaper publisher and columnist

THE FROZEN TRAIL

by Lisa Dayley

WiDō Publishing • Salt Lake City

WiDō Publishing
Salt Lake City, Utah

This book is a work of historical fiction. Although based on actual events, the author has taken liberty with various characters and dialogue for narrative purposes.

Cover by Tom Milan

ISBN: 978-0-9796070-4-2
www.widopublishing.com

Dedication

This work of historical fiction is dedicated to the members of the Willie Handcart Company. These courageous pioneers showed heroism and dedication in the face of unbelievably harsh and brutal conditions while en route to Zion to join their fellow Latter-Day Saints. It is especially dedicated to Willie Handcart member, Emma Girdlestone, who left behind a legacy of bravery, fortitude, and dedication; and who, 155 years later, managed to change the life of her great-great-granddaughter Lisa Dayley, the author of this book.

CHAPTER ONE

It's so warm in here. Those were Emma Girdlestone's first thoughts as she burst into the house.

It had been another chilly English winter, and Christmas Eve was no exception. Twenty-year-old Emma, the second of eleven children, placed her coat and mittens on the banister. She gathered her skirts and raced up the stairs, finding her family gathered around a new piano.

That piano was Papa's gift to Mama, and Mama had scolded him for it. "Thomas, I wanted to buy for the children," Mama chided as her hands flew up and down the ivory keys.

"Aw, yes, Mary, but I know any gift I give ye always comes back tenfold for the children," he said. He hugged her against his chest and kissed her lightly. The younger children giggled as they watched their parents' display of affection.

Emma looked on in amazement. How could he still hold her like that? Why was she acting like such a school girl after all these years and eleven children? Emma wondered.

Papa walked over to his favorite chair and leaned back comfortably. The flames from the fireplace flickered behind him. "Now play us a tune, my sweet," he said.

Taking notice of Emma, Mama smiled. "Emma, how nice to see you."

Emma scooted next to her mother on the piano bench and helped turn the sheets of music as Mama played.

Emma's frozen hands brushed against her mother's. "Emma, Luv, You're so cold. Where have you been?" Mama asked.

"Outside, in the snow," Emma said as she blew on her hands, hoping to warm them.

"James, get Emma a blanket," Mama told the oldest child as she continued playing.

As James hurried off to find a comforter, Mama turned back to the piano and continued playing. Emma resumed turning page after page. Her family sang along, loud and off-key.

"You know, Emma, we must hurry," Mama said with such calm Emma thought she must be joking. "We all must hurry. The bugle has called."

Emma moved closer to her mother, hoping to warm up a bit as she caught a draft that became increasingly colder. "But Mama, what bugle? What do you mean?"

Her brother James delivered a heavy blue flannel blanket, which Emma wrapped tightly against her slender frame. It didn't help; she was still freezing.

"Emma, my Luv, the bugle has called." Her mother smiled, gently urging her on.

The cold wasn't affecting Mama long fingers, which continued gliding up and down the keys. "Emma, the bugle has called."

Emma, shivering, looked out the frost-covered window of her home in Great Melton, England. "Mama? Why do I feel so cold?" She shut her eyes tight and wrapped the blanket tighter around her tiny five-foot frame.

"Come along, Emma," Mama whispered.

Suddenly Mama's delicate notes crashed and clashed together louder and louder until all Emma heard were grating off-key notes blasting into the air. "Mama?"

"Emma, come on. Will you please get up? Can't you hear the bugle?"

"Why are you yelling at me? Stop it," Emma moaned.

"We don't have all day," the voice called again.

Emma struggled to open her frozen eyelids. She labored to sit up, but her attempt to stand landed her face down in the snow. Her face was so numb she hardly felt the frosty snow.

Emma wiped her eyes, and, through the haze, she realized she wasn't in her warm home in Great Melton. Gone was the warm fire, the piano, and her mother. Instead, Emma was camped along the lonely windswept plains of Wyoming.

"If somebody don't get that girl moving, we'll be lucky to get anywhere by nightfall," the company wagon master, Captain James Willie, called.

"I try get her avake, but she keep calling vor her mum!" Bodil Mortensen, Emma's young friend, yelled back to Willie.

Bodil, a young Danish convert, was just nine years old. She had left her family in Denmark to trek to Zion with the Nielson family. Bodil's oldest sister, Ann Margrett, was already in Salt Lake, and would tend Bodil once she reached the valley. The rest of Bodil's family planned to head west that spring, so they wouldn't be separated from Bodil for long.

Emma and Bodil became fast friends as they trudged along. Emma helped Bodil tend the Nielson's little boy, Niels, who Bodil treated as if he were her own son.

"You'll make a wonderful mother, Sister Bodil," Emma assured her.

While the camp rested, young Bodil often scurried about making sure there was enough fire wood to keep the Nielsons warm. She helped make the biscuits that the famished pioneers devoured after a long day on the trail. And she often stood over a flame, stirring soup that helped wash down those biscuits.

Now Bodil tended to Emma. Bodil looked at Captain Willie who, in his haste, had forgotten that Emma's mother, Mary, had died.

"Oh, her mother. The poor lass," Willie said quietly, remembering Mama's passing. He threw the handcart company's few remaining supplies into the back of his wagon.

"No food, not enough blankets, eating that blasted rawhide soup; it's easy to forget the dead when the living are skeletons themselves." He threw another load into his weather-beaten wagon.

"Emma come. Ve both getting left behind," Bodil urged her friend.

"I'm sorry," Emma whispered as she struggled to stand and wrapped her soiled blanket around her. "I thought I was in Melton." Emma looked at the dirty threadbare blanket that had been so comforting in her dreams. Sadly, she shook off the dream of Great Melton.

Looking around the snow covered plains, Emma wondered if she would ever be warm again.

She gathered her blankets and followed the increasingly small band of cold and hungry pioneers on their way to settle the west. They were going to Zion, to Utah: the "land of milk and honey." Where it is warm, Emma thought longingly.

Emma watched as the mothers and fathers coaxed their little ones along. The orphans who had no one to help them. The widow and her children. The old widower, so terribly alone.

"Four hundred weary souls," Emma said as she brushed snow off her worn clothes and forced herself not to cry. The snow crackled beneath her shoes. Discarded cloth held her bedraggled footwear together.

Emma looked around for Papa and the rest of the family. Somehow all those little children managed to stay alive. James was just two years older than Emma, his hair as jet black as Emma's. He stood nearly six feet tall, taller and stockier than their father. The family used to tease James about his girth prior to the voyage, but now his clothes hung from his body. James helped his father as often as he could. He regularly rounded up the younger Girdlestone children, Little Thom who was seven years old, and Suzannah, who was five years old and the baby of the family, as they lagged behind. The two tots often sat down huddled together as the company traveled along.

"Come along now, Suzy," James urged Suzannah. "You don't want to get left behind."

The pair wouldn't budge from their resting place. No amount of coaxing from James inspired the youngsters to move. Nineteen-year-old twins Benjamin and John came to James' aid, lifting the little ones onto their backs and carrying them.

Benjamin and John looked so much like their older brother James; everyone thought the three brothers were triplets. Twins ran in the family.

"The Girdlestones come in twos; why not threes?" James joked.

The twins had lost much weight as well, and their suspenders, at times, seemed to be the only thing keeping their pants in place. Mama would be appalled at seeing her children in such ragged shape, Emma thought sadly. Yet, she marveled at how well Benjamin and James managed despite the conditions.

But they were farm boys, having grown up on the Hamilton Farm, working with their dad who worked as the farm's supervisor. Every planting season, they pushed plows and planted wheat. Throughout the spring and summer they yanked out massive weeds bordering the fields and hoed row after row of crops. During the fall, they harvested wheat by hand and stacked hay, always coming home well after dark, covered in sweat, dirt, weeds, and hay.

All that hay stacking put muscles on those boys, and that stamina now came in handy as they carried their siblings and pulled the handcart through the snow.

"Just pretend we're a haulin' hay," James quipped whenever he took his turn pulling the handcart. Papa begrudgingly let the boys take over. He stood along the trail catching his breath, but quickly caught up to his family and helped push the wobbly craft from behind.

Nine-year-old Jane often walked along with her seventeen-year-old brother Robert. They were the only redheads in the family and none too pleased about it. Robert's was especially red. Papa told Robert and Jane they got their flaming locks "from some Irish ancestor on your mother's side."

Robert was not amused. "I hate my blasted bloody hair. I'm no Irishman," he complained. "And Jane's no Irishwoman!"

"I'm English!" The offended Jane would stomp her feet.

Yet it was Robert's bright red hair, hanging from underneath his hat, that guided the rest of the Girdlestones when they lost track of each other during each blinding blizzard.

While the older boys tended to their younger siblings, fifteen-year-old William and thirteen-year-old Elizabeth pushed their family's handcart from behind. Eleven-year-old Sarah followed closely behind, her long black hair flying from beneath her hat as she struggled to keep up with her family.

"This handcart is such a bugger to move," William complained. "We get it unstuck only to get it stuck again."

"William, you mustn't swear," Elizabeth chided him.

Every few feet the pioneers blew on their frost covered hands. A mist enveloped them as their warm breath mixed with the frosty air. Mittens the Girdlestones wore at the beginning of the journey had long since been worn to threads and discarded.

On more than one occasion the girls had ripped cloth from their underskirts to wrap around their siblings' swollen, frostbitten hands.

"We'll be naked by the time we're done," Elizabeth giggled as her underskirts got shorter and shorter.

"We'll freeze to death while their hands stay warm," Sarah added.

Seeing his children struggle, Papa reminded them of their heroic ancestor Owain Glyndwr, who defended the Welch against invading armies, which resulted in uniting the country. It had been a huge source of pride for his mother, who was a direct descendent of Glyndwr.

"Me mum always told me, 'There's nothing you cannot do, Thomas,'" he recalled as he pulled the handcart through several feet of snow. "She'd say 'it's the Welsh in ye,'" he bragged.

Every time Papa repeated the story of Glyndwr, the Girdlestone children were both amused and annoyed.

"Papa has gone mad," William whispered.

"I don't want to hear about Glyndwr anymore," Sarah complained.

The family plodded through the snow, their shivering as constant as their breathing. Every conversation was broken up by trembling and shaking. So used to the discomfort, it was as if none of them had ever experienced warmth or an unshattered sentence.

Papa's constant reminders of "the Welsh in ye" now turned more desperate, like a plea, or a prayer that somehow his children would make it to Salt Lake. Mama hadn't made it. Now she lay buried out in the middle of nowhere. No word or stone marked her resting place. It had been that way for weeks, fresh graves by the wayside daily.

Emma walked over to little Thomas. The young boy's face was bright red from the cold. His little body shivered and shook as Emma buttoned his jacket.

Emma marveled at the blue wool jacket Mama had spent hours and hours making. Knowing they would need warm clothing, Mama stitched clothing for her large brood to wear while walking to Zion.

The Girdlestones were paid in wool for their work on the Hamilton's farm. While the Girdlestone men toiled away on the farm, Mama and her daughters spun the wool into yarn to knit mittens and make jackets. Mama stayed up well into the evening, sitting next to the fireplace, stitching mittens and sewing colorful jacket pieces together while her family slept.

Emma struggled against the cold to button Little Thomas' filthy, snow-covered jacket. Rags covered his hands. He shook against the cold but managed a smile.

"Without me jacket, I'd be more frozen cold," he shivered.

Emma smiled and kissed the tot on his forehead.

"We'll all be warm soon. 'Tis not far to Zion," Emma said as she hugged Little Thom, and hoped she was right.

CHAPTER TWO

Emma shivered against the October chill blasting its way through the valley. She heard Papa call to the youngest children. “Suzannah, Jane, Little Thom, come along now!” he shouted as the convoy of hand-carts formed. He waved for his children to join him. The snow cascaded around him in a flurry.

Papa rubbed his hands together and cupped them to his mouth. Steam rose around him as his breath hit his frostbitten hands. Papa smiled and nodded to Emma as he waved on his other children.

“Must keep a stiff upper lip for the children’s sake,” he whispered.

One by one, the younger ones made their way to the group. First came Little Thomas guiding Suzannah and followed by Jane. Sarah and Elizabeth tracked not far behind. James, Robert, John, Ben, and William trudged through the snow as they joined the group, preparing for another frosty day on the trail.

The Girdlestone children looked at Papa with confidence. Concern and worry showed through his eyes as he fought back tears. He kneeled to eye-level with Suzannah and fastened her dirty blue wool coat. "Button up them buttons. Get yur bonnet on snug, now, Suzy," he said softly. He was crying.

Emma knelt down and tied the string on Suzy's torn, filthy hat.

Benjamin picked up Jane and placed her on his back. She giggled as he plowed through one snowdrift after another. "Like walking through a Norfolk hay field," he joked.

That's all Benjamin had ever wanted to be—a farmer just like Papa. The two had spent many a summer harvesting crops, and now the Girdlestone men trudged through tundra that threatened to harvest them.

Just months before, the Girdlestone boys had planted wheat on the Hamilton farm. Now they looked forward to helping Papa on their farm in Zion. And it would indeed be their own farm, not one belonging to a rich British family, who, by the grace of God, allowed the Girdlestones to serve them. God had a farm for His servants in Zion.

The Prophet Brigham Young promised British converts their own land once they joined the "Great Gathering" in Zion. No more would they be beholden to anyone—no matter how kind or rich he was. They would be land owners.

"Papa, Benjamin makes a good pony, almost as good as Mr. Hamilton's pony. Remember how he let me ride old Sally?" Jane asked. "I would name it 'Her Majesty' after the Queen," Jane said.

"I wonder if Sally ever felt this cold and tired," Benjamin said as he rubbed his hands together.

Someday they wouldn't be so cold. Someday they would have their own ponies and horses. They would have their own land.

"Those boys of mine—they all bleed soil," Papa boasted.

The comment made Suzannah cry. Papa reassured her it wasn't true.

"Yur brothers bleed red like the rest of us, dear Suzy. No need to fret," he said, hugging her and patting her on the back.

The Girdlestones were destined to farm. Not one of the boys ever complained about the early mornings and the late evenings, and they never tired. Farming was God's chosen profession. The good Lord commanded Adam to till the soil, they reminded the women in the family whenever they came home covered with hay, muck, and mire.

"'Twas never a sweeter smell than sweat and dirt," James insisted.

"Aw, sweat and dirt, almost as pleasant as a daisy," William said.

"More like a rose," Robert added as they trudged along.

Emma turned up her nose at the suggestion. The four brothers laughed at the look on their sister's face.

"A city girl, you would be," Robert said.

Elizabeth and Jane planned to live in the city. "No more farm for me," Elizabeth said. "Jane and I are going to run our own clothing shop. Emma can make our dresses, and we'll sell them."

"A farmer's wife you're sure to be," Robert

joked as he raced toward his brothers.

The brothers plowed through the snow toward their family. Benjamin shivered a bit as he carried Little Thomas. His teeth chattered as he spoke.

"I feel like a pony. You need ta walk. Me back is a killin' me," he said as he put Little Thomas on the ground. The little boy ran through the snow, catching up to Jane.

"Benjamin is a makin' me walk too, Janey," Little Thomas shouted. He, Jane, and Suzannah played in the snow as if they were back in Great Melton. Their memories short, the snow and cold weather was their new home. Little Thomas picked up a snowball and threw it at his sisters, who lobbed one back at him. They quickly tucked their hands inside pockets to warm them. The pockets weren't much comfort. The youngsters' fingertips could be seen hanging out of holes.

As the younger Girdlestones played through snowdrifts, they spoke of their plans for the land of milk and honey.

"I'm going to be a cowboy, ride a horse, and fight Indians," Little Thomas told his sisters.

"You don't scare anybody. No Indian will be afraid of a little English boy!" Suzannah said as she and Jane laughed. Little Thomas chased after them, kicking snow into the air. The girls laughed as they outran him.

Suzannah and Jane planned on living in a big house from all the money they would earn from sewing.

"Emma will teach us how. We're going to get

rich, richer than the Queen of England." They both dreamed as they maneuvered through the snow. They picked up more snow, quickly turned it into a snowball, and threw it in Little Thom's direction.

Emma looked past her brothers and sisters through the crowd of tired faces. Strange how everyone in the wagon train looked alike. Seemed their faces were as white and expressionless as the snow they walked through every day. If pioneers weren't bent over from pulling a handcart for miles, they were hunched over from fighting the razor-sharp wind and mountains of snow.

She spied young James Kirkwood, of Scotland, just eleven-years-old, who always carried his four-year-old brother. That was his job while the boys' widowed mother pulled the family's handcart. The Kirkwoods often traveled with the Gadd family, another large family that made up the Willie Handcart Company.

James Kirkwood and Samuel Gadd were so close in age the boys had become inseparable.

Emma wrapped her dingy stringy scarf around her face and lowered her head against the snow. It seemed the snow blew sideways rather than straight down from heaven. She walked through the snow toward Elizabeth and Sarah. When she reached them, she straightened and tucked in the ragged leftovers of her sisters' scarves. Emma's hands were frostbitten and her shirt sleeves were covered with dirt. Her mittens, like everyone else's, were long gone.

"Emma, 'tis so frosty and cold." Elizabeth shivered as she slowly lifted her soggy shoes through the deep snow. Her teeth chattered. "We should have knitted some more mittens. Mama asked us to, but we thought we had enough."

We should have listened. We should have made more, Emma thought, and sadly shook her head. The Girdlestone women had indeed spent hour after hour knitting and stitching so late into the night, they could barely see what they were doing—the candle's light had fallen asleep as well. The sisters begged Mama to please let them go to bed.

"We have such a large family. We mustn't quit now," Mama reminded them. The girls picked up their stitching, yet often fell asleep in their chairs. They awoke to Mama gently ushering them into their beds.

"We may need more of these mittens. We'll start again on the 'morrow," Mama said as she helped her daughters into bed.

Dreams of stitching left Emma more tired than when she had gone to bed. Yet, she picked up her needles the next morning, stitching away again well into the night.

Mama had taught her daughters to knit and sew, just as her mother had taught her, and just as her mother's mother had taught her daughter.

"Someday, you'll thank me for this, my dears. Your grandmother told me the same thing." Mama smiled as the girls spun more yarn and turned it into jackets and mittens. "I didn't believe her."

Emma now wished for just a few more mittens. She wrapped an arm around Sarah.

"Guess Mama was right. I miss her. This blanket

she made is such a gift," Sarah said.

The frayed blanket Sarah wrapped around her shoulders flapped behind her as the wind whipped through the valley. The once beautiful quilted blue blanket was now weathered by snow storms.

"Thank heavens for this dirty ole blanket," Sarah shivered.

"Kissed by the angels," Papa said.

The bedraggled group pressed on. Papa pulled the handcart while his children took turns pushing from behind. The snow continued as the sun settled on the horizon.

Captain Willie rode up to the group and told them to make camp. "We can't make it any farther in this storm," he said.

No one argued. The Girdlestones stopped in their tracks. They grabbed their tent and blankets. The handcart groaned as if grateful its load had been lightened.

"It gets to rest as well," Emma said.

The Girdlestone men hammered stakes into the frozen ground. Papa beat the wood into the soil. He stopped to warm his hands. On the other side of the bedraggled tent, the Girdlestone boys struck the stakes several times with little success.

"The bloody blast—" Benjamin started to say.

"Benjamin, your language," Emma shushed him.

"Emma, it just won't go in the ground," he complained as he again beat the stake into the ground.

The pounding echoed through the night. The steady beat of hammers repeatedly hitting the wooden stakes was heard throughout the valley.

"Almost a melody," Emma said as she closed her eyes, "off-key."

"Emma, yur right. 'Tis a song," Jane agreed.

The frozen soil finally gave way enough to allow Papa and his sons to secure the stakes. The tents went up, swayed a bit in the wind and snow, but stayed put.

The family pulled more blankets from the handcart. Underneath the blankets lay Mama's dishes.

"All these fancy dishes and nothing to eat," Papa complained. Next to the dishes were Emma's vases that she insisted on bringing. Yet, for all his complaining, Papa continued hauling the heavy plates and vases to Zion, where it was warm and where there was warm food.

Tucked next to the vases was a tiny box holding a handkerchief Emma had made. "My treasure." She smiled as she reached inside the handcart for the handkerchief. Emma had made the "'kerchief"—as her father called it—as a young girl. Whenever the Mormon missionaries, Elder Dye and Elder Licorice, called on the family to preach, Emma stitched away as she listened. Emma had sewed around the white cotton handkerchief, emblazing the letter "G" on one corner of the hankie.

And it survived the trek from Great Melton to Liverpool and across the ocean on board the ship *The Thornton*. And now the handkerchief was safely tucked inside the handcart, protected from the wind, blizzards, and snow.

"It survived, just like us," Emma said as she

headed toward her family's tent.

So exhausted was everyone that little effort was made to make up what Mama would call "a proper bed." The Girdlestones threw comforters onto the frozen ground and quickly collapsed on top of the thin, dirty blankets. Papa placed some more blankets on his children before climbing under the covers himself. He mumbled a family prayer of gratitude.

The moon shone through the family's frayed tent, and Emma watched the snow fall hard onto the tent. As quickly as it landed against the wobbly structure, it quickly slid off. The steady rhythm soothed Emma's soul.

"Emma, your eyes are still open. Why are you looking up?" Jane asked.

"The snow is so cold but just so pretty," Emma said.

"It's noisy," Jane said as she rolled over on her side. "It's a poundin' on the tent."

Emma's eyes started to close, and the pounding that so annoyed Jane seemed almost musical.

"'Tis a lullaby," Emma said as she fell fast asleep.

CHAPTER THREE

Papa encouraged his young children as they pulled and pushed through the snow. He often let the youngest ride inside the wobbly handcart when the four older brothers tired of carrying them. The handcart's covering had long since been destroyed by wind, rain, and snow. It now sat in ruins atop the Girdlestones' possessions—barely covering the soiled items. What remained of the covering flapped in the wind as the family pulled it along.

As Papa pulled, he often lost his footing but just as quickly regained it. His shoulders hunched forward, his hands frostbitten from the cold, couldn't grip the cart very well. Rags replaced the gloves he had worn since starting the journey.

Sarah and Elizabeth pushed from behind as Papa yanked and pulled and coerced the handcart out of "another overgrown snowball," as he regularly said. He never failed to add: "I hope to never see another snowdrift again as long as I live!"

At the beginning of the journey, Papa had been "a regular ox." Papa pulled that wobbly handcart through deep sands, towering grass and rocky mountain ranges. He seemed never to tire and often let his younger children climb inside the handcart.

"Are yur feet sore? My poor little ones," he cooed whenever Suzannah and Little Thomas grew weary. He gently kissed them on the forehead. "Let Papa give you a rest."

Emma marveled at her father's ability to pull that cart stacked "bloody high" with all the Girdlestones' goods and "Mary's bloody dishes" and "Emma's bloody vases." Yet, he was a farmer used to hard labor, working from dusk to dawn stacking hay, harvesting grain, and wrestling with one obstinate cow or sheep after another on Mr. Hamilton's farm. The activity put muscles on Papa's tall stocky body, and he regularly beat other farmhands in wrestling matches.

"That'll teach ya for daring an old man!" said sixty-two-year-old Papa after winning matches against younger hired hands.

"A handcart is a bit like pushing a plow," he said. Every spring he tilled the soil while his sons joined him nearby planting wheat, barley, and hay. It was difficult keeping the oxen in line and the plow steady, but Papa always got the crops planted.

"Now I know how the ox feels," he joked. The tiny craft maneuvered through such rough terrain that it was a miracle it had survived at all. Those handcarts had proven very little help for most families. Built too late in the season, they often broke down along the trail.

Emma vividly recalled the shock on Mormon

officials' faces when she and five hundred fellow Willie Company pioneers arrived in Iowa City earlier that summer.

"We weren't expecting you! No one told us you were coming," they said as they raced around camp spreading the news about the unexpected Willie Handcart Company's arrival. But there were no handcarts available; it was too late in the year. "We are out of supplies! What were you thinking leaving this late in the year?"

Just earlier that month, President Daniel Spencer and other camp workers had outfitted the Edmund Ellsworth Company and its 274 pioneers. Two weeks later, on June 9, they had sent off Captain Daniel McArthur and his group of nearly three hundred. Captain Edward Bunker and his Welsh converts followed close behind, leaving June 28.

The supplies for that travel season had been exhausted. Spencer was at a loss for what to do. He paced, he worried, and then started the Willie Handcart emigrants to work sewing tents. Fortunately, much of that work had been done while the company sailed across the ocean on the ship *The Thornton*. The tents could be finished in time, Spencer hoped.

It was on May 1, 1856, that the Girdlestone family and the Willie emigrants left England on *The Thornton* for the New World. A month later the Willie group arrived stateside where they passed through the Castle Garden Emigrant Receiving Station before climbing aboard a Dunkirk, New York-bound train. From there they headed to Harmony, Pennsylvania, dividing themselves up into groups of eighty onto six train cars. There they sat, two on each side of the isle. Railroad workers had placed a stove in the middle of each car and at the end of each train car were restroom facilities.

"Everyone can hear you do your business," Emma whispered to her mother as she returned from using the bathroom.

Mama and her daughters packed food for the trip because train officials wouldn't provide any.

"I like your biscuits better, anyway," Papa had said as he ate the bread, scattering crumbs every which way.

The train rumbled through Harmony, Pennsylvania where the Mormon Prophet Joseph Smith did much of his translation of the Book of Mormon.

"Imagine we are just miles from where he held the Golden Plates." Emma envisioned the Prophet Joseph translating page after by page of the Golden Plates by candle light.

The older boys nodded off while the younger watched in amazement at the countryside whizzing by.

"It's like we're flying," said Little Thomas.

"We are a flyin'," Suzannah giggled.

"Like angels," Jane added as she looked out the window.

About 500 miles later, the pioneers were ready to board The Jersey City Steamboat to cross Lake Erie. Hundreds of people jostled their way onto the boat. The Girdlestones found themselves hanging on to each other and their luggage for dear life. Emma held her bags tightly to her body, hoping all that shoving and pushing wouldn't ruin her treasured vases she had packed so gently prior to the voyage. Those vases had been in the Girdlestone family for decades and had once belonged to Emma's grandparents.

Once aboard, the emigrant women headed down into the steerage where there was more room to accommodate the families. It was a cheap and unpleasant place—damp, dark, and crowded. Emma checked her vases, and Mama inspected her dishes for any damage.

Little Thomas, Suzannah, and Jane climbed up on their bunks and pulled the steamboat's flimsy blankets over them.

"Who would make such a blanket? Not much comfort to it," said Mama as she pulled out the blankets she had packed and covered the little ones.

In the meantime, the Girdlestone men and their fellow emigrants took to the deck and gazed out along the river. The sun shone down on Lake Erie. They stayed on the deck that day and through the next morning, thanking the good Lord for no rain or windstorms while they slept.

The next day the Girdlestones and their band of emigrants left the boat and rode the rails to Toledo, Ohio, later taking another train to Chicago. There they met an unpleasant conductor who didn't like Mormons on his train.

"You'll have to get off right here," he bellowed before they reached their destination. He opened the door and motioned the travelers to leave. They did so, finding themselves in the middle of the deserted

Chicago & Rock Island Railroad station. No lodging was available anywhere nearby. Emma looked toward the heavens and watched as clouds gathered above and lightning ripped across the sky. When the rain started falling, Emma covered her face and looked for shelter.

She followed Captain Willie and John Chislett as they searched the railway's buildings. Chislett and his fiancé, Mary Ann Stockdale, joined the company in England with plans to marry in the Endowment House in Salt Lake.

"Mary Ann is not so happy getting booted off the train," John Chislett told Captain Willie as they searched.

"Neither am I," Emma said as they looked in one building after another.

As the sun set, Emma, Willie, and Chislett anxiously looked for someone at the abandoned station to help them. It was well past five p.m. when the trio stumbled across an office with the words "Charles Perryman, Rock Island Railroad Station Superintendent" stamped on the door. Willie prayed as he knocked, and Perryman ordered him in.

"What is it?" he bellowed, noticing the threesome's worn clothing. He looked Emma up and down and smiled like a Cheshire cat. Emma looked away.

"Sir, I am with a group of…" Willie said as he took off his hat and held it in front of him. He looked from Perryman to Emma and back again.

"Yes, I know. You're one of them Marmons. What is it with all of you? Following after angels and golden plates and visions out to The Territory?

Are you mad, man?" Perryman rattled as he moved toward Emma.

Willie and Chislett moved closer to Emma.

"Sir, we were dropped off here, and we need someplace to stay for the night. There are several hundred of us and numerous children," Willie pleaded.

Perryman watched Emma like an animal after its prey.

"Sir, I am with a family of eleven. We have little children with us who can't be out in this storm," Emma said, and as much as it repulsed her, she gazed into his eyes, acting as though she found him the most handsome creature on earth. She batted her eyes.

Perryman looked into her eyes and then at Willie and Chislett. He softened a bit, returned to his desk. He grabbed a match and lit his pipe. He kicked his legs on top of his oak desk and slowly took a puff. The smoke encircled him. Willie waited for Perryman to respond. Emma kept her gaze on Perryman, growing increasingly uncomfortable at her fake interest in him. Finally, Perryman cleared his throat. He stood and walked toward Emma, blowing another wisp of smoke directly into her face. Chislett raised his fists, but Emma stopped him. Perryman looked outside his window. He watched as the emigrants sat on their bulging luggage. Many held weepy children in their arms as the rain cascaded down. Others joined in a circle with their heads bowed in prayer. Perryman pointed to a neighboring building.

"All right then, there's an empty warehouse just yonder," he said as he looked at Emma and pointed toward the old wooden structure just a few feet from his own building.

"Thank you, Sir. We are indebted," Willie said.

"God will bless you." Emma smiled and curtsied as Chislett grabbed her arm and escorted her out of the room.

"More suited for pigs than people," she said under her breath as she followed Willie and Chislett.

"We must all be thankful in all things," Willie said.

Emma hurried toward her family. She looked up and saw Perryman watching the pioneers encircle Willie. Captain Willie pointed toward the dilapidated building, and Emma helped gather her family's things. As she headed toward the building, she felt Perryman's gaze, but she didn't look back.

"The dirty old man," Emma mumbled as she helped her family carry their luggage into the building.

The Girdlestones unpacked their bedding and curled up next to each other in an effort to stay warm. Suzannah cried out and held onto Emma's skirts as the thunder roared and heavy raindrops landed on the flimsy wooden building.

The next day, the Girdlestones boarded the Rock Island Express headed toward Pond Creek with just half the group. There wasn't enough room for everyone, and the rest of the group would have to wait, Captain Willie explained.

When they arrived at Pond Creek, the bridge had collapsed. The rest of the company arrived shortly after midnight. With nowhere to go, the Saints turned their train cars into sleeping quarters.

In the morning, the travelers found plenty of food to resupply. Neighboring farmers were more than happy to sell fresh milk to the weary emigrants.

"'Tis good for the soul," Papa said as he sipped milk delivered straight from the cow. "It reminds me of Hamilton's farm." His children eagerly gulped down the first milk they had had in days.

Word got out that the Mormons and "plenty of women" were trapped on that train with nowhere to go.

"Hey, you pretty little thing. Don't go to Utah, stay here with me and be my wife," was yelled repeatedly as men gathered near the bridge. An anxious Papa quickly unloaded his family's luggage from the train cars, handing them to his sons, who loaded them onto a ferry which would hopefully get them to the Promised Land. Repairs to the track would be slow in coming and traveling by train was now out of the question.

Emma looked toward the bridge. The bright sunlight blinded her, and she raised a hand to her brow. She watched as the dirtiest and most foul Americans she had seen gathered on the bridge.

"Keep an eye on your sisters. Don't let them out of your sight," Papa ordered his older sons.

The boys moved near their mother and sisters. Little Thomas, now the little man, scooted toward Mama, wrapping his arms around her and clutching her skirts protectively.

Mama heard the catcalls and gathered Emma, Elizabeth, and Sarah to her side. Young Suzannah and Jane scooted toward their older sisters.

"They are indeed evil, miserable men," Mama told her daughters.

"And ugly to boot," Emma said as she watched the men spit tobacco. Tobacco juice streamed down their faces, and the men wiped it off with their filthy shirt sleeves.

Papa guided his wife and daughters toward the Ferry. The Girdlestone boys, carrying the family's gear, followed behind.

William turned to see the jeering crowd move closer and closer. "Papa, I think we had better hurry," he said as he ushered his sisters along. Emma's heart pounded as she watched her father and brothers. James, William, John, Ben, and Robert dropped their luggage loudly onto the ground.

"Enough is enough," James said.

The boys faced the agitated crowd. Other husbands, fathers, and brothers from the company formed a tight circle around the entrance to the ferry. The Willie Company women stood protectively within the circle.

A gunshot was fired.

Emma whirled around to see the town's sheriff and deputies approaching on horseback. They rode toward the unruly crowd who was just a few feet from the ferry boat.

"You men, now get! Now get out of here!" ordered the sheriff as he fired another shot in the air and then slowly lowered his gun toward the crowd. His deputies drew their pistols, aiming them at the rowdy mob.

"You damn sheriff!" cried one man as he spat out some of his tobacco toward the sheriff and his deputies.

"What are you? A Marmon lover?" another shouted. "You want them little ladies for yourself?"

The deputies moved closer to the mob, keeping their guns pointed at the rowdy bunch. The crowd continued hollering at the Willie Company travelers.

"There's a mess of sweet young things just awaiting you. Brigham Young can't have 'em all," another sneered.

The sheriff fired a bullet through that man's hat, knocking the man to the ground. The remaining troublemakers grabbed their hats and ran off, leaving the emigrants to load their luggage in peace.

"Jesus must have sent the sheriff," Little Thomas said as Emma guided him onto the ferry.

"Indeed he did," Emma said in relief, offering up a silent prayer of thanks.

At last the Willie Handcart Company arrived in Iowa City. In Iowa City the railroad ended, leaving anyone who wanted to go farther west to rely on horse-covered wagon and handcart.

A pouring rain greeted the travelers as they exited the train. They found shelter in an outbuilding close by. Emma helped herd her younger siblings inside the building. The structure offered protection from the rain, but it still proved a cold night. The Girdlestones once again wrapped themselves in Mary's soft blankets.

The next morning, the emigrants trudged toward

the Mormon Camp. As they entered, officials ran to and fro, shouting at one another.

"We don't have any handcarts ready. It's late in the year," they kept repeating. "Why weren't we told you were coming?"

CHAPTER FOUR

The pounding wind and snow brought Emma back to the present. She stopped to rub her hands together for warmth.

Emma hadn't done much of the pulling since the heavy snow storms had struck. Seeing her father struggle, Emma offered to give him a much needed rest. Papa insisted on pulling the family's handcart while his older children pushed from behind.

"No, Emma, I can do it. I've pulled it this far," Papa said.

"Papa, you're exhausted; let me pull for now, please," she persisted as she stood in front of the handcart. Papa tried going around her every which way with the handcart, and each time Emma blocked him.

"Just walk for now, Papa. No more pulling for a bit," Emma said as she cupped her hands, covered in scraps torn from her dress, and blew into them before picking up the handcart. Through the threadbare material, she felt the cold crossbar.

"Just a wee bit frosty out," quipped James from behind.

“We’re cattle,” she shouted. James smiled and mooed as he shoved the handcart from behind. William and Robert raced over to help him get unstuck—again.

“I think the cows are happier,” James joked.

Emma struggled to pull the handcart while her brothers pushed from behind. The snow was like the sand had been during the summer. When the handcart got stuck in the dirt, the family pushed it forward and backward again and again before finally digging it out of the dirt with their bare hands. At one point Papa and the boys had lifted the handcart up and out of a sand dune.

“’Tis as if Satan is reaching from the depths of hell and holding on to our little handcart,” Emma complained as she knelt next to the handcart and scooped handfuls of muck away from the wheels.

“On the count of three!” Papa shouted as the Girdlestone men lifted the wheels half buried in the sand. Now the sand was replaced with snow, and the task of pulling the handcart was twice as difficult. Emma noticed Papa’s face become increasingly pale and weary. She watched him hobble along. The snow got deeper and deeper and every step required more strength than the last. Papa’s steps slowed and his feet faltered.

“What if gangrene has set in?” Emma fretted as she pulled the handcart along.

With the ongoing snow storms, pioneers were finding green and black splotches covering their feet, arms, and legs. Too much exposure to snow and rain and no chance to properly dry off made the pioneers susceptible to gangrene where tissue died after too much contact with wet weather.

Emma remembered when one of Mr. Hamilton's farmhands had spent days in muck on the farm without having a chance to dry off or get a decent bath. A doctor visited, and after taking one look at the appendage, proceeded to amputate the farm worker's diseased foot. The physician gave him whisky to numb the pain and a piece of wood to bite down on as he sawed the foot off below the man's ankle.

"Grit down," the doctor ordered the man. The farm worker bit down on the wood but screamed anyway as the little piece of lumber fell to the floor. The racket caused the younger Girdlestone children in adjoining rooms to cover their ears and hide.

Emma shivered at the memory. Several members of the company cringed as they slowly lifted one badly infected leg and then the other through the snow. Many lay down for several minutes until a fellow pioneer picked them up and placed them inside a cramped handcart.

Emma's friend, Ella Nielson, became so tired that at one point she refused to move one step farther.

"I can't. My leg hurts. I'm too cold," she complained to Emma. She showed Emma her leg. "My skin is black and green," Ella said as she leaned against a rock and wrapped her arms around her shivering body. Emma said nothing about the leg.

"If I say anything, she'll just give up," Emma thought. "If she knows what I know, she'd stop in her tracks. She'll lose her leg."

Ella and Emma, so close in age, became fast friends early in the journey. Ella traveled with the

Olaf Wickland family, of Denmark, helping care for their young children. But now, Ella was in no condition to help anyone and could scarcely help herself.

Seeing her distress, Emma put the handcart down to help make Ella comfortable as she rested. Just as Emma placed the tiny craft on the ground, Papa raced to pick it up.

"I got me rest," Papa insisted. "Hand over them reins, missy!"

Emma turned to Ella. "Rest now. I'll be right back." Emma raced through the snow to find Olaf Wickland. The snow blurred Emma's vision as she searched for Olaf through the crowd of pioneers. Everyone looked the same. They were black figures struggling against an icy white background, bent over, fighting the blustering wind, and pulling handcarts, a moving mass through a curtain of snow.

"Excuse me, Brother, do you know where Brother Olaf is?" she asked around. Each shook their heads. One finally pointed toward the front of the group. Emma smiled her thanks and caught up to Olaf.

"Ella is refusing to move another inch," Emma said, shivering between each word as she tried to catch her breath.

"I vas vorried. Ve hadn't seen her." Olaf's voice trailed off as he lowered his handcart. He walked around the handcart and dug through clothes, supplies, and cooking utensils until he pulled out a buffalo blanket.

"This should help," he told Emma. "I'll be right back."

Olaf headed toward the back of the company with Emma following close behind. Emma and Olaf knelt beside Ella as she shivered. Emma folded the blanket over and around Ella's body.

"It's like I'm tucking her in," she told Olaf. Ella gradually stopped shivering as the warmth generated by the heavy buffalo blanket sent her into a deep slumber. "This will give her a chance to rest for a bit," Emma said.

Emma and Olaf caught up to their respective families. As the company continued on over the plains, Emma slowed her pace, expecting Ella to catch up with the rest of the group. Nearly an hour later, still no Ella. Emma headed back down the trail to find her.

Emma ran past the last of the pioneers.

"Ella! Ella!" she called.

Emma raced down the trail, scanning the landscape for her friend. As she ran and shouted, Emma tripped over what she thought was a snowdrift. Emma fell, and just inches from where she landed was Ella, enveloped in a pile of snow.

"Ella, wake up," Emma ordered as she shook her friend awake.

"Emma?" Ella said, wiping her sleepy eyes. Warmth had returned to Ella's cheeks, and she had stopped shaking.

She struggled to stand as Emma grabbed Ella's arm and helped her to walk. The two friends slowly followed the Willie Handcart Company.

"Can you make it on your own, Ella?" Emma asked.

Ella clutched the buffalo skin around her and nodded.

Emma released her hold on her friend, brushed back her long black hair, and rushed toward her father struggling with the handcart. She stopped Papa and grabbed the handcart's crossbar again.

"Now now, Em, I can keep a pushin'," he argued.

Emma shushed him as she held the crossbar up, allowing her father to climb out from underneath. Papa hesitated and reluctantly clambered from below.

"I can keep pullin'," he struggled to say.

"No more." Emma shushed Papa as he started arguing. With the handcart out of his hands, relief washed over his face, and he leaned against a giant evergreen.

"It's the Welsh in ye. That's me Em, always a willin' to help. You let that James help ya out a bit," he ordered. "William and Robert are as strong as oxen, they can take their turn."

Emma picked up the handcart, hearing her vases and her mother's china rattle.

"All those fancy dishes and nothing to eat," Emma laughed as she mimicked what her father had said dozens of times before. She couldn't part with the dinnerware, the last remnant of their nice warm home where food was a plenty. She felt fortunate that Papa had let her keep the possessions instead of tossing them along the trail. Many fellow travelers dumped unnecessary items along the trail to ease the weight of the cart.

"One man's treasure, soon his trash," Emma

marveled as she witnessed heavy, unnecessary items being discarded.

"The handcarts can take only so much—as can we," Papa said.

Emma sighed as she felt the Wyoming wind slice through her worn clothes and increasingly slender frame. Skin and bones is what Mama would say. Emma's eyes scanned the frozen prairie, and, looking behind her, saw her siblings trudging along the trail. Despite the rugged conditions, the younger Girdlestones did remarkably well. The older boys carried the younger children, who pretended their brothers were ponies.

"Giddy-up, Benjamin! We'll get left behind!" teased Jane as she kicked him in the sides.

"Let's gallop," Suzannah urged James. "James, you're not as fast as Mr. Hamilton's pony!" Suzannah joked.

"I'd like to see that pony out here," James shot back.

James pulled Suzannah from his back and yelled at Emma to stop. He handed the little girl to William and pushed the handcart. Elizabeth and Sarah joined James in shoving while Emma guided the handcart through the frozen grounds. Razor sharp winds cut through their clothing and ragged mittens. Thin and unraveling knitted scarves wrapped around their necks, covering their faces but doing little to protect them from the elements. And for every step they made falling snow and blizzards forced them back two more steps.

Emma marveled at James' resilience. No matter

how cold and blustery, and no matter how hungry and tired he was, James always helped. Just twenty-two years old, he acted like a father to his younger brothers and sisters, giving away most of what Emma gave him to eat. He gathered the little ones up each night, and, just like Papa, counted heads while Emma made dinner.

Since arriving in the territory in August, the travelers had relied on hard-tack biscuits, but now all that remained were dusty flour bins. No longer was there any flour to make biscuits. Instead, they relied on soup, the bones from butchered cattle providing marrow to what otherwise would have been boiled snow water. But it wasn't enough to sustain any of them. At night Emma fretted and fussed over what to feed the family.

Emma prayed, and as she opened her eyes, she spied some rawhide still attached to the handcart's wheels. She blew on the animal skins, hoping to thaw the material as she yanked.

"Come on, you bloody rawhide!" Emma growled.

Ella limped toward her friend and extended a hand. "Let me help you."

The two young women pulled at the rawhide, winding it off the frozen wheels. The last yank sent them flying into a snowdrift.

"Hunger made us strong," Emma laughed. The young women stood and brushed snow from their coats. "Ella, take some. I know the Wicklands are hungry too."

"It's a feast for the queen herself," Ella said. She

hobbled and limped back to the Wickland's camp.

Emma headed toward her family's campsite, where she scooped up handfuls of snow and tossed it into the kettle. Papa and the boys spent nearly an hour on their hands and knees blowing onto wet wood.

"That blasted wind kept a blowin' it out," James complained after the men finally got the fire going.

"It's God's gift that it started," Papa said. The family gathered around the flame that thrashed and wiggled in the determined wind.

While the family warmed themselves, Emma tossed strips of rawhide into the snowy mixture. The water quickly turned brown as it boiled around the hardened animal skins. When the soup was ready, the family gnawed the animal skins with their front teeth until the rawhide turned white, stringy, and soft. They drank cups of snow water to wash down the leather. Emma didn't tell her family that the meat had been rolling across the ground for hundreds of miles. She sipped just a bit of the gooey mixture. James poured some of his soup into Emma's bowl, but she quickly pulled her bowl away, shaking her head.

"I know where you got this meat!" he said. A surprised Emma looked at her brother, but she bit her lip. James poured what he had into his younger siblings' bowls. "I don't care how hungry I get; I'm not going to eat that damn rawhide soup."

Papa caught him and poured his own soup into James' bowl. "You better eat. It may not be good food, but it's food, for Heaven's sake. Now eat."

Papa noticed Emma's reluctance to eat as well. "Em, you've got to take something. We need you.

This soup is better than nothing." He handed her a bowl, but she pressed it away.

"I'll spoon feed you if I have to. You know, sweet Em, it hasn't been that long since yur Mother and I did this for you as a baby," he said. He brought the spoon to Emma's mouth, but she grabbed the utensil out of his hand and fed herself. Suzannah yelled for Papa, and as soon as he was out of sight, Emma offered her soup to Bodil Mortensen, who had joined the Girdlestone family for the evening. "Have the rest," Emma offered the girl.

Bodil gobbled it down. "Be happy for zee food, Sister Girdlestone," she said. "Zee Bible says to be grateful for all things. I am most thankful for you and yur soup."

It was indeed food. It was warm—the only warm, thick substance Emma had known for days. She admitted it did make her feel better.

"'Tis my humble pie." She lifted what was left of the soup to her mouth.

CHAPTER FIVE

While Emma forced down her portion of the rawhide soup, Papa and his older sons struggled to erect their tent.

The wind howled and blew. Each time the Girdlestone men raised a side of the structure, the wind knocked it down as if an unseen arm took a swipe out of the sky. But the Girdlestone men eventually secured the tent's ropes to the stakes, managing to keep the tent upright.

Emma and Ella had spent hours stitching that tent together. Patience Goodfellow, "the company's busybody," as Emma called her, had made sure of that.

"If you don't keep a stitchin', we'll never make it to Zion, and it will indeed be your fault. Hurry, hurry, hurry. Stitch, stitch, stitch!" After days of Patience barking orders at everyone, Emma had had enough.

"Not one more stitch." Emma held out her throbbing, bleeding hands. Her fingertips were cracked from so much sewing and handling the rough canvas. "I can't, Patience."

"We must hurry and finish. We must prepare for our journey." Patience plopped more canvas at Emma's feet. "You must keep sewing, Sister Girdlestone. You must hurry, or we will never ever reach Zion. We'll never meet the Prophet, never go the Endowment House, and never ever make it to the Celestial Kingdom because you were slothful. Now you must sew, sew, sew. What would your mama and papa think if they could hear you a complainin' like a spoiled little princess? If I was your dear parents, I would be so ashamed of you." Patience stormed off onto another errand.

"My parents want me to play the piano, not destroy my hands for the likes of you," Emma cried as Patience walked off to order other women about. Emma's friend Ella had watched the exchange between the two women.

"Aw, Emma, don't let her get to you. She has no sense, and she's just anxious to leave. She has too much spirit and not much compassion." Ella dipped a rag into a cool bucket of water and wrapped the cloth around Emma's swollen hands.

Now Emma looked at her hands, taut in the frigid temperatures. Instead of being stiff from all that tent sewing, they were now stiff from the cold. She flexed her fingers, wincing with the effort. She wondered if she would ever sew or play the piano again.

All that canvas Emma had stitched now proved to be a lifesaver for her family and her fellow travelers.

"Without my tent, dear Sister Emma, I don't know what I would have done," said Margaret Dalglish, who traveled alone. Whenever Emma felt she couldn't pull the handcart another inch, Margaret appeared out of nowhere pulling her tiny craft along without complaint.

Margaret often joined the Girdlestone family, or "The Brits," as she called them, each night for supper. She seemed as hungry for companionship as she was for food.

"Your family, I don't know what I would do without them, Sister Emma," she said as Papa and James helped Margaret put up her tent. "I am indeed grateful."

Fellow travelers straggled into camp. Many clutched blankets around their thin frames.

"Famished beyond words," Margaret sighed.

"And not vell. Not vell at all," said Bodil Mortensen, who joined the Girdlestones at their campsite.

Travelers with handcarts carrying those too sick to walk pulled into camp.

"I don't know how any of us made it up this trail," Emma said as she helped secure Margaret's tent.

"Indeed, it has been a difficult hike," Margaret agreed as she tightened a rope around another stake. Her handcart lay slumped on its side as if it were exhausted. "A sorry sight indeed."

While Suzannah, Little Thomas and Jane gathered kindling, Papa and his older sons started a fire. They bent down on the ground and blew onto the struggling flames. Bedraggled pioneers trudged silently into camp.

John Chislett helped the weary travelers along. John hadn't suffered as badly from the harsh elements as others. Youth was on his side.

"You were sent to us from God. I don't know what we'd do without you, John," Captain Willie said, patting him on the back.

"Come along now. Just a little further until you can set up camp," Chislett said as he urged pioneers onward and upward. Many looked as if the next step would be their last.

It was as if their souls had been frozen. Emma handed Margaret some rawhide. "Please, Sister Margaret, throw some of this meat into the pot. We can share this. If you could help me fix something for my family to eat, I'd be most grateful." Emma turned back down the trail. She greeted each traveler who moved closer to camp.

"There you go, you're almost there," she said, urging them along. They muttered a word or two of thanks as they continued trudging through the snow, bent over, yanking their carts along the difficult trail.

CHAPTER SIX

It continued snowing through the night. The next morning, after pulling up camp, they followed the winding Sweetwater. Chunks of ice floated down the river. It would be the third time in three days that the company had been forced to traverse the frosty Sweetwater.

Willie ordered the men to organize their families. "We'll need some volunteers to help the widows and their young ones. Where's John Chislett? Somebody, help me find John."

One by one, handcarts and wagons entered the icy rushing waters. John Chislett helped ease the pioneers into the freezing waters. "Steady now, miss. There ya go. Won't be long until you're safe on the other side."

If that tiny Irish woman can cross the Sweetwater, again, than surely I can too, Emma thought as Margaret Dalglish slowly walked into the river crossing. The Sweetwater knocked Margaret about, but as soon as she was halfway across, she had no more trouble.

"A strong Irish lass," Emma said as she watched Margaret finish her watery voyage.

Fellow pioneers helped fish her from the river.

"A bit frosty," Margaret said as she climbed out of the water.

"Your turn, Sister Emma," John Chislett said, helping her into the freezing water. An ice chunk floated past. "Aw, Brother Thomas. Let me help your little ones." John Chislett waded back to shore.

"Thank the good Lord for you, Brother John," Papa said, pulling his family's handcart through the churning waters. At times the water reached his waist. Papa steadied himself on the slippery rocks as the Sweetwater rushed by.

Emma carried Little Thomas while James followed with Suzannah. Papa made it ashore and quickly grabbed Little Thomas from Emma. She gathered her skirts and slipped up the embankment until gaining her footing on the snow.

When James was almost ashore, he held Suzannah out to Emma. But before Emma could get a hold of her sister, James slipped, sending himself and his little sister cascading into the cold water. As the waters rolled over Suzannah, she vanished.

"Suzannah! Suzannah!" James screamed as he thrashed about in the water.

All movement across the river ceased as attention focused on finding the little girl.

"We've lost one in the river!" Chislett cried as he raced down the banks of the Sweetwater, searching for Suzannah.

Eleven-year-old James Kirkwood and his friend

Samuel Gadd raced past Chislett along the banks of the river. James Kirkwood yelled as he and Samuel jumped in the river. Up they came from the icy waters and dove back in, each time coming up empty handed. They swam farther down the river, diving into the Sweetwater.

James Girdlestone half-swam, half-ran after the boys. He dove into the icy water. He only came up to catch his breath before diving back in. Papa followed. Chunks of river ice knocked into the men. "Poor little Suzannah. 'Tis so cold," Emma cried as she solicited heaven that her sister wouldn't be buried in a watery grave. Men ran down the banks of the Sweetwater, searching while women followed, carrying dirty worn blankets to warm the girl should she be found.

James Kirkwood yelled, emerging downriver. Samuel followed close behind. Water dripped from their drenched clothing. James carried the limp Suzannah in his arms. He shivered as the Wyoming wind blasted through the valley. Emma raced toward them.

White as a ghost, Suzannah struggled for breath as Emma took her from James. Suzannah coughed out a few words as water spilled from her mouth.

"Mama? It's frozen cold," Suzannah cried.

"I saw her go under. I thought she was gone but downstream she bobbed up for a bit. Sam saw her blue bonnet. We weren't going to let her go." James Kirkwood sobbed. "I caught her right before, right before she went down," he said as he struggled for breath.

Captain Willie raced down to the riverbank. He reached for Suzannah, wrapping a comforter around her.

"Poor little one," he said. He handed the girl to her weeping father.

Papa cried as he kissed Suzannah's forehead. He hugged her, then handed her to Emma and headed back to the rest of his family crossing the river. Papa carried Jane and Little Thomas to safety. Back and forth he and James went, helping anyone who needed assistance.

Papa carried the widow Mary Ann Williams across the river. He went back and carried her sixteen-year-old daughter Eliza across as well.

"I can cross by myself," insisted the fourteen-year-old son as he headed into the river. When he fell in the icy water, Papa scooped him up and deposited him on the other side. The stunned boy nodded his thanks. James arrived on the bank carrying Mary Ann's two daughters.

James Kirkwood and Samuel Gadd continued helping pioneers cross the Sweetwater. The Willie Company labored past nightfall to bring the 400 travelers across the rough river. Once everyone had crossed the Sweetwater, pioneers found themselves at the base of Rocky Ridge.

"We should be further along," Willie fumed as he kicked his wagon. He paced anxiously, then busied himself helping travelers start their camp fires.

Emma hauled a kettle to her family's campfire. She tossed some snow into the pot and looked through the handcart, hoping to find enough flour to make some kind of a soup. She prepared a meal with some leftover flour stuck to the floorboards of the handcart and a little rawhide.

So little food and so much need. Rawhide and the bones of cattle were their only source of nutrition.

The company started its trek with thirty-seven beef cattle and eleven fully stocked wagons. Willie required that each handcart carry a hundred pounds of flour. The weight caused some of the travelers to complain.

Willie called a meeting urging pioneers to stop grumbling and thank their Heavenly Father for His divine help and intervention on their behalf.

"Brothers and Sisters, we must replace the spirit of grumbling, strife, and disregard of counsel with the spirit of gratitude," Willie counseled. "If you are asked to pull four hundred pounds of flour in your handcarts, you must pull it cheerfully. Our milk cows can't carry any more weight. I am asking each of you to put extra flour inside your handcarts," Willie said.

While many of the pioneers murmured at burdening their wobbly handcarts with more flour, John Chislett walked over to one of the wagons and grabbed a sack of flour and put it in his handcart.

As Captain Willie talked, John Chislett filled his cart. By the time he was done, five hundred pounds of flour weighed down his handcart.

Papa followed John's lead, and before long, fellow travelers were adding extra weight to their handcarts. That extra weight, however, affected the already wobbly handcart wheels. On more than one occasion Papa had to stop and jury rig the handcarts heavily burdened axels to keep them turning. As the flour was eaten, the handcart became easier to pull.

"What I wouldn't give to have all that flour now," Emma said as she looked across camp, watching mothers make do with rawhide and very little else. They needed energy to climb the 750-foot Rocky Ridge on the morrow.

CHAPTER SEVEN

As the bugle called the next morning, Emma roused herself. Tripping over sleeping family members, Emma reached for the tent's flap. She peeked through the opening and looked upward at the enormous Rocky Ridge. They would be knee deep in snow and blindsided by a ferocious wind. Emma saw others readying themselves for the hike.

While she surveyed the countryside and Rocky Ridge, her family awakened.

"Emma, you're lettin' the cold in!" Little Thomas complained.

"We need to get up and get a movin'," said Papa.

They packed everything in the handcart, and the little ones huddled together for warmth as the family made their way to the base of the mountain. There they found Levi Savage inspecting the peak.

"Brother Savage. It isn't your fault. We should have listened to you," Emma said. "I am sorry that I didn't."

"You're most kind, Sister Emma," Levi said as his teeth chattered on every word that left his mouth.

He helped Papa lift the Girdlestones' cart out of a snowdrift.

Emma felt a wave of guilt, remembering the night in Nebraska when she and her family had voted to continue on to Zion. Mama might still be alive had they listened to Levi's warning.

As the wind whipped about her, Emma recalled how tensions mounted among the group that night.

"Papa, remember how much we fought against Brother Levi?" Emma said as they trudged along.

"That meeting is something not to be forgotten," he said. "Brother Levi tried to stop us. The Holy Ghost spoke through him, indeed."

"And we failed to listen," Emma said.

She recalled Captain Willie holding a company meeting where everyone stated their piece about whether to continue on to Salt Lake. Levi had warned the crowd: winter was coming. Their clothes were too thin. Their shoes were already worn out. Captain Willie asked for a vote and the only one opposed was Levi.

"Yet he promised to help us. He said, 'Brethren and sisters, what I have said I know to be true, but, seeing you are to go forward, I will go with you and help you all I can,'" Emma remembered. "'I will die with you. May God in his mercy bless and preserve us.'"

Now the wintery conditions were worse than Levi had predicted. She turned to Levi.

"Brother Levi, not once have you condemned us for not listening to your promptings. You were the only one listening. You are a blessed Saint and blessed with the Holy Ghost," she said.

"There is no reason to condemn," Savage said. "The Holy Spirit still guides us. The Savior, I believe, is still with us." He moved on to help another family with their handcart.

Emma again faced the mountain. Rocks jutted out here and there. Ice formed along its side. "This mountain has truly earned its name. Rocky indeed," she said.

CHAPTER EIGHT

Weary travelers stumbled as they passed Emma on their way up Rocky Ridge.

She raised her hand to her brow and watched as the company fought against wind, sleet, and snow while pulling their handcarts up the icy rock-covered mountain.

Papa pulled up next to her.

"'Tis rocky, to say the least," he said, letting the handcart rest for a moment. "Brother Levi was right, but I didn't believe it could ever be so bad," Papa said as he tended to little Suzannah. He moved the family's meager possessions around the craft to help make Suzannah more comfortable. The rest of the Girdlestone children passed by, heads bent down and arms folded across their chests.

"It won't be long until Brother Richards sends help," Emma assured the family.

Just weeks prior, Apostle Franklin Richards, returning from a mission in England, had stumbled across the weary group. Richards promised that a rescue party would help them finish the journey, but they must keep going.

"You need not worry. You are God's chosen people," he told them.

When the apostle visited, the pioneers had gathered around to hear his words of encouragement. He reminded the pioneers of the handcart program, and how it was inspired by the Prophet Brigham Young. It would save new converts money and would bring them to Zion much faster.

"I don't think oxen could have done the job better than meself." Papa picked up the handcart and moved forward. "I feel I'm stronger than an ox on Mr. Hamilton's farm. I could outwork one right now!"

Why had so much gone wrong for them? Emma forced her own confused feelings aside.

"Papa, remember they did say they would send help," Emma said as they continued up Rocky Ridge.

"Yes, they did promise. We mustn't worry," Papa said.

Emma recalled Elder Franklin's promises: "You must be patient. You must be prayerful, and you must be obedient to the priesthood at all times and at all costs. Yet, I am concerned about you. I know you have struggled, but, Brothers and Sisters, I promise we will send supplies to help you along the way."

Those words now echoed through Emma's mind as they continued up Rocky Ridge, trudging through twenty inches of snow and pulverizing wind.

The Girdlestone men rammed the craft over jagged rocks jutting out of the snow. Those rocks often tumbled onto fellow pioneers, and their cries could be heard from below. Apologies shouted through the wind weren't heard. Emma held tightly to Jane and Little Thomas' hands. The wind yanked the children's scarves away from their little faces, and every few steps Emma stopped to rewrap the material again and again. Suzannah curled up asleep inside her family's handcart, oblivious to her father's struggle in climbing the ridge. Captain Willie's blanket enveloped her entirely. When the handcart hit a bump, Suzannah stirred and called out for Mama but just as quickly fell back to sleep.

Little Thomas and Jane grew too weary to walk, so Benjamin and James picked up the tots and carried them on their backs. The youngsters clung tightly to their brothers. This time there was no pretending the older boys were ponies. Their young eyes peered over their brothers' shoulders as they maneuvered the rocky landscape. Elizabeth and Sarah hiked behind, their arms folded across their bodies, their heads down as they fought the wind and snow.

Pioneers trekked to a summit, only to have gravity pull their handcarts down into another small valley.

Up and down Rocky Ridge the company went. Suzannah's rescuer, James Kirkwood, trudged nearby carrying his little brother Joseph. The younger boy's arms hung tightly to his big brother's neck.

"Not much farther, Brother James," she said, but James Kirkwood answered with not a word. He kept his head down as he climbed over rocks, sometimes slipping, but not once did he drop little Joseph.

"Brother Kirkwood?" Emma said, moving

closer to James Kirkwood, but again he said nothing as he continued climbing, holding tightly to his little brother.

For the next five hours Emma's company hiked the ridge. Scanning the terrain she saw John Chislett running back and forth helping pioneers move their handcarts over snowdrifts and rock piles.

"Don't give up. Keep a moving!" he urged the pioneers. "You've not got far to go." His shouts were scarcely heard over the blasting wind. Travelers cried as they stumbled, but Chislett wouldn't let them quit.

"You mustn't stop. Come along now. You can do it," Chislett shouted as he helped push their handcarts out of the snow. "Not much farther to go."

The Girdlestones were one of the first families to reach Rocky Ridge's summit. They pulled out the tents that Emma had stitched while in Nebraska.

Sarah and Elizabeth searched for kindling while their brothers raised the tent. They pounded stakes into the ground while cursing the soil.

"You blasted bloody frozen ground," Benjamin yelled. He continually hit his hands while hammering, yet his fingers and hands were so frozen, he hardly noticed when the hammer hit his hand and when it hit the stake. Emma reached for his hand but found that neither the skin nor the bones had been broken.

"It's too cold to break," Benjamin joked. "It's too cold to bleed."

"Indeed, it is," Emma said as she rubbed his hand, hoping to warm it a bit.

"No need. I'm fine," he said, pounding the stake.

Finally, the soil gave way and the Girdlestone boys could secure the tent.

"We did it, Benjamin!" James shouted, patting his brother on the back. "That'll teach this countryside to mess with Norfolk boys."

Elizabeth and Sarah staggered through the snow, hunting for wood. They found a bush poking from underneath the snow. The girls broke off pieces of wood, yet they returned with just a handful.

"It was all we could find, Papa," Elizabeth said.

"No buffalo chips to be found here," said Sarah.

Those buffalo chips initially sickened Emma. The unusual American way of starting campfires had to be the most disgusting thing she had seen along the trail.

"A proper British lady would never pick up such a thing—not if her life depended on it," she had said.

"Ah, but Emma, this isn't Britain," Papa reminded her. "And our lives do depend on it."

Emma cringed as she had helped pick up the only source of fuel the pioneers could find along the trail last summer. Thousands of buffalo lived along the prairie, and the pioneers gathered the hardened buffalo manure like it was gold.

"A big cow's stinky helping us to stay warm," Little Thom laughed.

"It's revolting," Emma said, but had a change of heart when she realized those buffalo chips actually helped get the fire going.

In the midst of all that snow, Emma would have given anything for some buffalo chips to start the fire.

"They really were like gold," she said. She

wandered from the campsite and found a smattering of wood and handed it to Papa.

"Praise to God for His mercy," Papa said about the small amount of wood. He and his sons got down on their hands and knees to blow on the kindling. Their worn rags scarcely covered their hands.

"Come on, now," William said as he blew on the campfire.

"Keep a prayin', boys," Papa said.

A small flame began and twisted and whipped about against the ferocious wind. Grateful the fire had started, the family knelt in a prayer of gratitude.

"We must be grateful for all things, Sister Emma," Margaret Dalglish said as she joined the family around their campfire. The flames suddenly roared. "It's like it wants to spite the wind."

"Finally, some warmth. Indeed, we must be grateful," Emma said, bowing her head in prayer and asking that Brother Richard's rescue teams arrive shortly.

CHAPTER NINE

On October 4, 1856, a dirty Franklin Richards arrived in Salt Lake City just as the semi-annual Mormon Conference was about to start.

Since finding the pioneers, Richards and his fellow missionaries had rushed to Salt Lake, sleeping just a few hours each night. Each day they urged their horses and cattle to go just a little faster. Two weeks later, the men arrived in Salt Lake just in time for the Mormon conference, where the Prophet Brigham Young and his apostles would dispense God's counsel to His children.

Richards didn't stop at home to clean up. He rode straight to the Tabernacle, where he raced to the podium where the Mormon Tabernacle Choir was singing, and Prophet Brigham Young sat with the apostles. "Excuse me. I'm sorry. Excuse me, Brother," Richards said as he brushed past apostles to reach Brigham Young.

"President Young. The Willie Handcart Company—" he gasped out. Richards clutched his filthy hat in his hands. "They're headed toward the

Valley. It's late in the year."

Franklin Richards felt eyes boring into his back. He shuffled nervously as he awaited Brigham Young's response.

"You need to take a breath and calm down, my dear brother. What has you so troubled?" Brigham Young asked.

"The Willie Handcart company," Richards said, struggling for breath. "We caught up to them in Nebraska. Their handcarts are falling apart. They're most assuredly in Wyoming now. I don't know if they can continue on much longer."

Young looked at Richards as if he'd lost his mind.

"What handcart companies? What are you talking about? I didn't authorize any handcart companies this late in the year," Young exclaimed. "There were no handcarts scheduled for October. It's much too late in the year to be traveling through the mountains."

"We must get help to them soon," Richards said.

Brigham Young placed his hands on Richards' shoulders.

"Bless you, Elder. Those pioneers in the mountains will be helped. We'll get a rescue party organized right now," he said.

Franklin Richards hurried off the podium and waited near the exit as the choir sang.

Brigham Young rose from his chair and hushed the choir. The confused choir members stopped one by one. The organ music faded as the singing trailed off. The Prophet announced that there was a convoy of saints headed toward Salt Lake.

"At this moment, many of our brethren and sisters are on the plains with handcarts. They may be seven hundred miles from this place. We must send assistance to them. We must get them here," he said. He rested his hands on the podium.

"All your faith, religion, and profession of religion will never save one soul of you in the Celestial Kingdom of our God unless you carry out just such principles as I am now teaching you. Go and bring in those people now on the plains. And attend strictly to those things, which we call temporal or temporal duties. To God there is no difference between temporal or spiritual. All are one and the same to him. Otherwise, your faith will be in vain. The preaching you have heard will be in vain to you, and you will sink to Hell unless you attend to the things we tell you. President Richards is waiting for your help—he can lead us to these people."

Young dismissed the conference and turned to his counselors to help organize the rescue party. October marked the end of the annual harvest, and this year had been a successful one in the Salt Lake Valley. The crops brought in plenty of money to outfit the people with everything from clothing to food. They had been blessed and had plenty to share with the stranded pioneers. Men from the meeting gathered around Richards.

"I've got a team of horses and a wagon I can get ready right now," said one man.

"I've got a team as well," volunteered another.

One little girl shoved her way into the growing

circle of men surrounding Richards. She stretched her skinny arm toward him and handed the Apostle her raggedy doll. "For a little girl, who's lost all her poor little dollies," she said.

Richards, busy talking about rescue tactics, took the doll and nodded his thanks.

Women headed home, where they searched through closets, grabbing dozens of unfinished quilts. They cut and tied the quilts. Their children had never seen the ladies work so quickly. Usually the mothers chatted, taking time to finish quilts. This time, the women silently stitched and tied.

The women, carrying bundles of blankets, headed toward the wagons. Their children followed behind carrying clean clothing, coats, socks, and food. Rescuers loaded wagons with so many supplies that the supplies bounced out as they headed toward Wyoming. Youngsters ran to pick up the goods and waved for the men to stop, but the rescuers, in their haste, continued on their journey. Nobody knew what they would find, and nobody knew whether the pioneers were still alive.

Wives and children waved the men on and returned home, where they prayed for the rescuers' and pioneers' safety.

In one home, a little girl prayed that her doll would find "a little girl just like me." As she finished her prayer, it started to snow.

CHAPTER TEN

As the snow beat down on Rocky Ridge, the Girdlestones were on their knees praying that rescue parties would soon find them.

"They've got to be out there somewhere," Emma cried as travelers stumbled into camp.

James Kirkwood staggered into the encampment with his brother Joseph still clinging to his back, his arms practically frozen around James' neck. Emma helped Joseph slide off his brother's back. James silently lay down not far from the Girdlestones' camp.

"James quit talkin'. He's a layin' in the snow with no blankie," Joseph said to Emma.

When Margaret Kirkwood arrived, Emma, James, and Papa helped her set up camp. As the Kirkwood children gathered wood, Papa and James stoked the campfire.

"Thank you so much, Brother James, Brother Thomas, Sister Emma. I do so need the help," Margaret said.

Emma grabbed a blanket and gently placed it

over James, lying silently in the snow.

"The poor lad is worn out," she said.

As Emma made rawhide soup for her family, Bodil Mortensen came up the path to join the Girdlestone family. Margaret Dalglish soon followed, dragging her wobbly handcart and joining Bodil at the Girdlestones' campfire.

"I finally caught up to your family, Sister Emma. It was a long trek indeed," Margaret said.

"I haven't seen you in quite avile, Sister Emma. I vas vorried, very vorried about you," Bodil said as she and Margaret warmed their hands at the Girdlestones' camp fire.

"The devil might have placed the mountain there, but the angels have helped us along the way," Margaret said.

"'Tis a comforting thought indeed," Emma said as she handed soup to Bodil.

Margaret stared into the fire.

"You know, Sister Emma, I looked behind me, and I know it may sound like—as you Brits say—like I've gone mad, but as I was hiking up the mountain, I didn't think I could go another step, but I did. I looked behind me, and I swear I saw—what would you call it? A ghost, an angel? Something or someone helping me push. I wasn't doing it myself. I was getting some help from above, I do believe."

"The Spirit of our Heavenly Father has been helping us all," Emma said.

"Jesus helped me," Little Thomas added.

"Indeed, he did, most certainly," Bodil said as

she watched Papa struggle to keep the fire going.

"It luks like ve need more firevood." Bodil stood to leave, but Emma reached for her little hand.

"Bodil, please, don't go. I beg you. We've got enough for now," Emma said as she tightly held Bodil's hand. "It's so cold. You need to rest. You all need to rest."

"Sister Emma, ve need some more vood," Bodil insisted, shivering as she struggled to stand up. She yanked her hand out of Emma's. "I be vite back. Some vood nearby. I'm sure of it."

Margaret tried stopping the girl as well. "Bodil!" She reached for the young girl, who headed toward some brush. "That girl is one stubborn Dane," Margaret said.

"She's as stubborn as you, Margaret!" Emma said as she clutched her blankets around her. "She must have Welsh in her as well."

Bodil headed toward some wooded overgrowth and waived at John Chislett as he approached the Girdlestones' camp.

"Sister Bodil," John greeted with a tip of his hat.

Chislett turned to Papa.

"Brother Thomas, we need your help. We've lost a dozen people this evening. We need help burying them," Chislett urged. "I hate even to ask, I know you're exhausted, but there are so many. Would it be too much trouble?"

"You're such a fine young man. Emma oughta marry you." Papa winked as he stood to help John Chislett.

Margaret laughed when Chislett turned red.

Emma blushed. “He’s engaged to Mary Ann!” she said.

Chislett met his fiancé Mary Ann Stockdale through the Mormon missionaries while living in England. After becoming engaged, they joined the Willie Handcart Company.

“We were too poor to buy a wagon,” Chislett had told Emma earlier. “I want to save the money and take Mary Ann on a decent honeymoon.” Mary Ann never complained as her intended spent most of his time helping others along the trail.

Papa and John left the Girdlestones’ campsite and began the grim task of gathering the dead. James followed, and Emma soon joined them. She shivered as she trudged through campsites with the men, collecting frozen corpses. Both the young and the old had succumbed to the conditions. No one was immune.

“The life goes out as smoothly as a lamp ceases to burn when the oil is gone,” John Chislett said, looking at the frozen bodies. Even those who just hours before had seemed so healthy and robust were now frozen.

Family members made not a whisper as the bodies of loved ones were quickly and quietly removed.

“You will see your loved one again. There will be a reunion during the resurrection,” Emma told them. “The Prophet Joseph promised us that families continue far beyond the grave.”

In all, the men retrieved eleven bodies. John Chislett, Papa, and James struggled to dig a grave into the frozen ground.

"I can't get it any deeper." James beat at the snow-covered dirt.

"It's as solid as rock," Emma said, and whispered a little prayer that Heavenly hands would soften the soil. "These bodies can't be buried in snow." She looked around the campsite and watched families struggling to start campfires.

"That's it!" Emma quickly turned to the men.

"We need to build a fire. It's the only way, the only way to loosen the soil."

The group split up to gather what little kindling they could find. Across the campsite, she found a few twigs. The frozen bare tundra didn't offer much in the way of wood, and Emma wondered if Bodil had any luck finding kindling. Emma scanned the frozen landscape and noticed a lone tree jutting out of the ground. Emma rushed toward the tree, tripping over her raggedy skirts. She struggled to stand and wiped the snow off her dress. She grabbed a branch at the base of the tree and leaned on it until the limb broke. She plummeted forward, landing face down in the snow. She stood and gathered the extra pieces of wood that had broken from the tree before heading back to camp.

She found Papa, James, and John Chislett carrying twigs and branches. The men threw the wood onto a pile and rubbed wood together to start the flame. Gradually the fire took hold and crept heavenward.

John Chislett grabbed his shovel and continued digging, with little success.

Emma looked toward the corpses. Among the dead were several useable shoes.

"Those could be worn by the living. We need those shoes so badly," Emma whispered to John Chislett.

"There is such a need. I've had to do that before," he said.

It had become increasingly common for burial workers to remove useable clothing for the living company members. No one wanted to take clothing from the dead, and this party was no exception. Yet Emma bent down and removed the shoes from one unfortunate traveler.

"Like robbing a grave," she said as she unbuckled a pair of boots.

"Aw, Sister Girdlestone. 'Tis a grim task indeed," John Chislett said.

John Chislett helped remove clothing from the corpses and told Emma of traveling on the South Pass and burying a pioneer whose footwear was still sturdy.

"I looked at them and at my own worn-out boots. I wanted the dead man's shoes so badly, but could not bring my mind to appropriate them," he said as he took a shoe off of one corpse.

"I can see why you wouldn't want to," Emma said as she stood up, walked a few feet, and threw up. She wiped her face with snow and dried it on her dirty dress. Emma returned to the grave and again removed clothing from the dead.

Emma removed a shoe from a man she recognized. His name was Chesterman Gilman, a widower from England who had adopted everyone as his grandchild.

Papa removed a jacket from a deceased company member.

"'Tis a grim task, to say the least," Papa said and tossed the jacket into the clothing pile.

"The poor man, but he'll never be cold again. He's in the warm presence of his Savior and his Heavenly Father."

John Chislett grabbed his shovel to resume digging. Emma watched him pound at the soil that started loosening, thanks to the fire. Emma continued removing shoes and socks from the dead. The warm flames softened the soil, making it easier to dig. The men shoveled enough dirt to create a mass grave. "We can put them three or four abreast and three deep," John Chislett said.

Emma continued removing footwear and gently removed the boots of William James, who had guided his family of seven children up the ridge. And there lay Elizabeth Bailey, the farmer's wife who left behind a seventeen-year-old daughter. Next to Sister Bailey lay James Kirkwood and his friend Samuel Gadd—little Suzannah's rescuers. "Not both of them," Emma cried. She stood and turned away. She paced as her father and brother continued digging. John Chislett stopped for a moment.

"Emma, no one's to blame. Those boys wanted to help. It was just too cold," he said. He leaned on his shovel. "It is not your fault. It is not Suzannah's fault. The Lord prompted them to help, and now they are with Him. He called them home."

"The poor lads. They saved my Suzannah," Papa cried.

"Samuel couldn't stop shaking after the Sweetwater. I watched him by his family's campfire. He shook all night long. The Sweetwater, it was just too much for him," John Chislett said and bowed his head in prayer.

Emma wrapped her shawl around her shoulders and shivered as she scanned the row of corpses. Emma looked at each dead pioneer but froze when she found her friend Ella among the dead.

The gangrene had gotten to her.

"Not Ella," Emma sobbed as James lowered the dead woman's body into the ground.

The names of the departed continued, and there lay young Niels Nielson, Bodil's young charge, just two days shy of his sixth birthday. Emma knelt beside him. It was so cold, and he was so little. Emma saw Niels' shoes, still useable, but little Niels Nielson would keep his shoes.

The men lowered the little boy into the ground, then the bodies of James Kirkwood, Sam Gadd, and Chesterman Gilman were gently placed in the grave.

Despite their efforts, the grave couldn't contain all the bodies. The men continued digging away at the sides, but the further they got from the flames, the harder the soil.

"Let's put one or two crosswise at the head and feet of the others," John Chislett said.

Not one of the dead pioneers' families attended the burial. There were no solemn scripture readings and promises of eternal glory. There were no more tears to shed. The burial was taken care of quickly and quietly.

"If they just could have held out a wee bit longer," Emma said.

"It just got too cold. So very very cold," John Chislett said.

As the men shoveled dirt and weeds over their dead companions, Emma felt her stomach churn. She ran behind a handcart to regain her composure. Behind the handcart, Emma found Bodil Mortensen curled in the snow, clutching a handful of twigs.

Emma shook the girl. "Bodil?" she urged.

There was no response.

"Bodil!" Emma cried. "Wake up. You must not go to sleep. Let's go sit by the fire. That will warm you up."

Emma kneeled down and gently shook the little girl. Again no response. Emma checked under Bodil's nose for a breath. There was none. She pressed her hand against Bodil's back. Again there was not a breath drawn by the little girl. Bodil was dead. Emma picked up the little girl and staggered toward Papa, James, and John Chislett. She slipped on the snowy ice, nearly dropping Bodil's body, but quickly regained her footing.

"Papa!" Emma cried as she carried the small body. Papa hobbled toward his daughter and saw young Bodil.

"I found her lying next to a handcart. She looked like she was sleeping, holding her bundle of sticks," Emma said.

James and John reached for young Bodil's body.

Removing some of the dirt from the mass grave, they gently laid Bodil's body next to the other corpses.

"It is a shame, but they're with their Heavenly Father. They are no longer cold and hungry." Papa smiled at the comforting thought.

Emma looked up the trail and for a moment she caught a glimpse of young Bodil and Niels. They were no longer cold and starved. They waved goodbye.

The family made their way back to camp. As John Chislett headed to another campsite to help a family restart its flame, he shouted, "Brother Thomas, Brother James, you must rest. I can't thank you enough for your help. The Lord will bless you for what you've done. I'll take care of the others."

Papa and James joined the rest of their family around the campfire. Emma grabbed two remaining blankets to warm the chilled men. How Papa managed to bury the dead when days prior he had forged rivers was more than Emma could fathom.

"It's the Welsh in ye," was all Emma could surmise.

Papa and James seemed to relax as the younger Girdlestones snuggled next to them. Little Thom and Suzannah huddled together.

"Papa, I'm frozen cold," Little Thom cried.

Papa and James' presence hadn't disturbed Suzannah, who, since her fall into the Sweetwater River, continued to say very little. She stared into the campfire flames as Emma secured a blanket around her shoulders.

All of Mama's old blankets, once filled with soft

batting, had been replaced with frozen clumps of dirt. Hardly much comfort any more, Emma thought.

The youngsters seemed content to just stare into the flames. Emma threw more snow into a pot and peeled rawhide from their battered handcart. Emma thought of poor little Bodil as she shredded the rawhide.

Emma looked around the camp at all the families.

"They're all so cold—frozen cold," she said, stirring the soup. "Why has God forsaken us? Where is He?" she cried, and was instantly ashamed.

Emma scanned the campsite and noticed all the families without their mothers. She watched another family with their father and watched children without either parent. And then there was John Chislett, so helpful to everyone.

"What would we have done without him?" she wondered. Emma smiled at the thought of Papa trying to marry them off.

"I don't think John's fiancé would much appreciate the thought," she mused.

Yet, despite the horrid conditions, no one seemed angry. They all just seemed thankful to be alive.

Emma tended to her soup, dumping more snow into the pot and tossing in what little rawhide she had left. Disappointment washed over her as she recalled all that was promised her family if they joined in the Great Gathering in Utah. Elder Dye and Elder Licorice, the missionaries who had converted her family, had given glowing reports of Zion.

"We just should have stayed put in Great Melton.

We could have served the church there instead of being trapped here on this God-forsaken mountain," she grumbled.

The missionaries explained that Utah was the land of milk and honey and warmth. It was the land of which the Prophet Joseph Smith had foretold and promised to be a place of peace for the persecuted Mormons. God would rule, and everyone would be of the same faith. Zion was to be found in Utah, where all would be well, and there would be great joy. Everyone would be of one mind. It would be Heaven on earth. Yet what Emma had seen over the past few weeks had been more hell than heaven.

"This is all my fault," she cried, and watched as her tears fell into the soup. "If I just hadn't insisted."

"Emma," came a soft voice. Emma whirled around.

And for a moment Emma forgot how cold, hungry, and angry she was. For a moment Emma saw Mama at the piano playing and singing with her family—loud and off-key. Images of the family packing up and leaving together filled Emma's mind. She witnessed the family hauling all their worldly items onto the boat. Mama's music crescendoed as the ocean waves lapped the ship on the sail toward Zion: The land of milk and honey—where it was warm.

"Emma, it's no one's fault," Mama said, looking directly at Emma. She turned back to her piano.

Emma watched her family singing in Great Melton. Then the image of Elder Dye preaching from the pulpit floated through her mind.

"The great gathering is of God!" Elder Dye declared as he pounded the pulpit, causing the children to jump.

"Oh, my goodness!" Suzannah had said, grasping her father's hand.

"He's noisy," Little Thomas complained as he covered his ears.

That image faded to reveal Emma's family reading from the Book of Mormon, then bowed in prayer.

"Blessed are we to have this scripture," Mama said as the vision floated away.

That image was replaced with seeing her family board *The Thornton* with hundreds of Willie Handcart members. Zion called, and the saints heeded.

Emma's rawhide soup boiled violently, splashing hot water on Emma's frozen hands, jolting her back to the present. She filled two bowls of soup for Papa and James.

"Here, I know you must be hungry," Emma said as she poured.

James and Papa, who just moments before had helped dig a mass grave, seemed to have lost all their strength. Both men shook uncontrollably. Emma secured blankets around them.

"It may not be good food, but 'tis food, for Heaven's sake," James mimicked his father.

Emma smiled as she placed a bowl in James' frostbitten hands. She placed another bowl in Papa's hands. He struggled to hold his bowl still.

"My Em," he managed to say through chattering teeth. "My sweet Em."

"Let me help you, Papa," she said.

Emma held the bowl of soup to Papa's trembling lips. He thankfully gulped it down. It was the first time he had eaten in days. Most of the rawhide soup slid down the sides of Papa's mouth and onto his wet clothing.

"Papa, you need to rest," Emma said. She threw another comforter on top of Papa, who grabbed it with both hands, holding it tightly around him. She did the same for James. The two men stared into the flames, but despite the warmth generated by the fire, they continued to shake.

"I'll take care of the little ones," she said as she helped Little Thomas, Suzannah, and Jane. She guided the youngsters into the tent where the older children had already started making their beds for the night.

"Papa, James, climb in here," Emma said. As Papa struggled to stand, Emma helped him up. James followed behind. The two men limped into the tent where Robert and Benjamin made a space. Papa collapsed onto the comforters, and Emma piled more blankets on top of Papa and James. She made a space for herself next to Suzannah and covered herself with a blanket.

"My sweet Em," Papa said as he closed his eyes.

CHAPTER ELEVEN

Captain Willie was out of patience.

More than a month had passed since Apostle Richards promised help, and the Willie Handcart Company was out of food. Willie paced back and forth. Bitterly cold temperatures and no food had turned the living into the living dead.

"Even the rawhide soup sounds like a feast," Emma murmured as she made more of it.

"Sister Emma, have you seen Brother John Chislett?" Captain Willie asked.

Emma pointed down the trail. As he headed past Emma's campsite, Captain Willie approached John Chislett.

"John, I know there's help out there. President Richards wouldn't let us down. I want to meet the rescue party halfway," Willie said. "I need you to watch over the camp."

Emma looked around at the increasingly desperate band of pioneers. She recalled earlier that summer and just six miles out of Florence, Nebraska, the company had spent the night singing and dancing. Many of the men had asked Emma to dance, and as she spun around, she watched as John Chislett and his fiancé weaved in and out of the crowd.

"A joyous bunch indeed," Emma had shouted to John Chislett as she and her partner danced past the couple.

"Such merry peals of laughter, Sister Emma," he said, and spun Mary Ann around. The two couples stopped for a moment to catch their breath.

"Sister Emma, it would appear that Brother Savage's warning has been forgotten by these happy pioneers in the ease of the hour."

"I tend to agree, but I see no bad weather on the horizon," Emma said.

Mary Ann grabbed John Chislett's arm.

"Oh, John, you worry too much. Bon mots, John, bon mots!" she said faking a French accent.

"A terrible accent, my darling," John said as he spun her around and around.

"Indeed a terrible accent," Emma joked as the couple danced past her.

Those days were a stark contrast to now as Emma's family struggled for warmth around their campfire. She watched Captain Willie and Joseph Elder saddle up their horses. Emma grabbed a few leftover biscuits she had retrieved from beneath the floorboards of the supply wagons and stuffed them into the men's saddle bags.

"Captain Willie," she said. "Are you sure you should leave in this storm?"

"Sister Emma, we can't wait any longer. If we

don't find help now..." he said, leaving the thought unfinished.

"God be with you, Captain Willie," she said.

Willie and Joseph Elder quickly mounted their horses. Willie turned to John Chislett to give some final instructions. "John, I'm counting on you to watch over the company while I'm gone. I know you won't let me down. I hope to be back in a few days."

"I don't know how much longer we can hold out. Death is stamped upon their faces," John said, shaking hands with the men. Captain Willie and Joseph Elder kicked their horses and sped toward Salt Lake. John Chislett looked around at the perishing group of pioneers.

"Sister Emma, the life of these pioneers is going out as smoothly as a lamp ceases to burn," he said. "We must pray that Captain Willie and Brother Joseph will find the rescue parties."

Emma watched as a woman shivered and gathered a soiled blanket around herself and her young child. The child clung to his mother's filthy, torn skirts.

Emma offered a silent prayer: "Father, please deliver this band of pioneers, your modern day Israel. Only through your grace will they survive."

CHAPTER TWELVE

Captain Willie and Joseph Elder headed into the storm, scanning the horizon for a rescue team. The landscape stared back, bleak and menacing.

"I thought for sure they would be here by now," Captain Willie said.

"The weather is against them, and our company is hidden by Rocky Ridge and a mountain of snow."

The wind picked up, and the two men buried their heads into their coats. The horses struggled up the ridge through drifted snow and rocky terrain. Captain Willie's horse slipped, causing him to slide off his saddle. He quickly righted himself.

"Steady there, girl," he said and patted the struggling animal.

Unable to hear past the wind, the men used hand signals to communicate. Snow continued to swirl around them.

While Captain Willie and Joseph Elder traversed the frozen prairie, the Salt Lake rescue party camped along the Sweetwater River. They huddled along a bank of willows for protection from the blizzard.

It was no use continuing. They had to wait out the storm. The blinding conditions would prevent them from finding anyone. In the meantime, Captain Willie and Joseph Elder ventured down the trail when they noticed an odd rock formation jutting out of the landscape.

As they got closer, they realized that it wasn't a rock but a signboard reading "Salt Lake Rescue Teams this way." A large black arrow pointed the way. They immediately whipped their horses in the direction of the arrow. The horses spewed snow heavenward as Captain Willie and Joseph Elder galloped into the rescuers' camp.

As they rode into the encampment, Joseph Ridges was headed back to his tent. Hearing the sound of horse hooves, he spun around and saw Captain Willie and Joseph Elder speeding into camp. Willie and Elder jumped off their horses and embraced the startled man.

"We are with the Willie Company. I'm James Willie and this is Joseph Elder."

"Thank the good Lord. We've been looking for you!" Ridges embraced the two men.

"The rest of your company, are they still alive?"

"Yes, they are," Willie cried. "And we need to get to them now!"

Joseph Ridges shouted and raced from tent to tent. "We've found them. They're still alive!"

Rescuers bolted from their tents, shouting with joy as they tore toward Willie and Elder.

"Thank God, you found us!" Captain Willie and Joseph Elder were embraced over and over again by the rescuers.

"We saw the sign and rode your way," Willie said.

"You saw my signboard?" Joseph Ridges struggled to gain his composure.

"It was your signboard, my dear brother that guided us here."

Joseph Ridges explained he couldn't sleep. He kept dreaming the same dream over and over again and got out of bed to make the sign.

"In my dream, I saw you. I saw you riding through the storm. I couldn't get your attention. I yelled and yelled, but you wouldn't stop," he said.

Harvey Cluff had hiked up a neighboring mountain to place the sign. "Was Hell a-frozen over," he said of the three-mile hike. "I had never been so cold." He told of fighting the blizzard all the way up the mountain. For every step he took forward, it seemed the wind pushed him back a dozen more.

Cluff said that after hiking up the mountain, he finally reached the summit, where he tore away the brush and rammed the sign into a massive snowdrift so it could be seen by anyone traveling down the trail.

"I slammed it so hard, I fell backward. I tumbled down the hill, but I could still see the sign," he said.

"Your sign saved our lives, and it will save my company," Captain Willie said. "Had we kept along the path, we would have missed you."

"Brother Richards, you kept your word," Captain Willie said to Franklin Richards.

"I am so sorry that you were caught in this

storm," Richards said. "We tried getting here as quickly as possible."

"The point is that you got here, and just in time," Captain Willie said, then turned to the others. "We ran out of food. We ran out of supplies. The handcarts are broken. We have many sick. They can't continue on alone. We've lost many along the way. They're starving. Our flour is gone. There is nothing left," he said.

Captain Willie looked at the dozens of fully stocked wagons. The rescue party's wagons were filled with clean clothing, blankets, and food. It was more food than Captain Willie had seen in weeks.

Several of the rescuers loaded their horses with supplies and took off on horseback. The remaining men tore down tents and extinguished campfires. They jumped into their wagons and quickly headed back the twenty-seven miles Captain Willie and Joseph Elder had come.

"We must pray for another miracle, Brother Elder," Willie shouted over the storm.

While the rescue teams raced toward Rocky Ridge, the Girdlestone family huddled in their tent, hoping starvation, snow, and freezing temperatures wouldn't kill them before help arrived. The warmth they generated made up for the lack of food. Eventually they fell into a deep sleep.

Suddenly Suzannah screamed out.

"Mama!" she cried.

Emma woke and saw a man in their tent chewing on Suzannah's feet.

"Get out, get out!" Emma screamed and beat

him back.

John, Ben, William, and Robert were now awake and they grabbed the man, tossing him out into the snow, where he lay still. Ben checked on him a few minutes later and found him dead.

Emma rocked Suzannah. "It's going to be all right, Suzy. The poor man didn't know what he was doing," she said.

The family hunkered down in their beds. Dreams of a warm Great Melton summer flooded Emma's mind. Mama sat at the piano playing while the Girdlestones sang. Suddenly Mama's music echoed into a chorus of heavenly instruments.

Chislett sounded the bugle.

"The bugle has called!" Emma cried as she shot out of her bed.

She lifted the tent's flap and looked outside. The sun had set, but along the horizon wagons appeared. Wagons loaded with supplies rumbled into the Willie Company camp.

Chislett sounded the bugle around camp.

"The rescue teams are here," he shouted.

"Is this Heaven? Men that don't look cold and famished? Oxen that aren't dropping dead? Sturdy wagons filled with supplies?" Emma rejoiced. "I must have died in my sleep," she said, rubbing her eyes. "How could Heaven be anything less?"

Little Thomas cried for Mama.

Everyone in the company dashed toward the Salt Lake wagons. Grown men cried while little children danced around the rescuers. Women surrounded the men and covered them with kisses.

"Restraint has been set aside in general rejoicing!" Chislett shouted as he hugged Mary Ann and kissed her.

Captain Willie jumped off of his horse and raced toward Chislett.

"John, we need you to set up a commissary. We have flour, potatoes, and onions. We have blankets—God bless the Valley Saints—we have blankets and buffalo robes and woolen socks. We need your help in handing these out," Captain Willie said.

John Chislett looked at the people, who just minutes before could scarcely leave their beds, dance around the wagons. Those who had been the walking dead the night before now ran toward the rescuers.

"The change is almost miraculous, so sudden has it gone from grave to gay, from sorrow to gladness, from mourning to rejoicing," Chislett chuckled. He shook hands with Captain Willie, and the two men embraced.

"Captain Willie, you made it! Thank the good Lord for His providence," Chislett said.

"I knew they had to be out there. I knew we'd find them," Captain Willie said.

Rescuers passed meat and bread to the famished travelers. Warm bowls of soup were passed out to company members who had lived off nothing but rawhide soup for weeks.

Suzannah brightened at each taste. She let each bite stay in her mouth for a couple of minutes before swallowing.

"Brother, is the food this good in Zion?" Suzannah asked Joseph Ridges.

"It's even better there," he promised, yet he urged Suzannah to eat slowly. "Your tiny tummy can't handle too much too soon."

Emigration officials had learned from sad experience that those who went without food for long periods of time often gorged themselves to death. Too much food eaten too quickly often overwhelmed the body and caused a quick death for those starving for months.

Captain Willie raced toward Emma's campsite. "Sister Emma, your friend Sister Vestenskov is in labor. Can you help? She's about to deliver."

Emma raced to Hans and Karen Vestenskov's tent, where Karen was in the last stages of labor.

"Aw Seester Emma, vee need yur helpa," Hans pled.

Emma had assisted her own mother in childbirth.

"Sister Karen, you've got to push," Emma encouraged as Karen Vestenskov leaned forward. Sweat poured down Karen's forehead as she panted. "I need towels! I need more warm water!" Emma said as the newborn left the warmth of Karen's womb.

"It's a girl." Emma rejoiced as the newborn's cry rang through the valley.

Despite the horrid conditions during the pregnancy, the baby was healthy. "Life after all that death," Emma mused as she cut the umbilical cord and washed the babe. Captain Willie hollered at the Vestenskovs and Emma through the tent's flap.

"May I come in? I have some clothes and a comforter," he said.

"'Tis another Daneesh babe," Hans rejoiced.

"Another babe of our Heevenlee Fauder so soon from zee speerit vorld."

"Name it after me!" Captain Willie joked as he entered the tent.

"Captain Willie, it's a girl," said Emma.

"Name her after me anyway," he said.

Emma left the Vestenskov's tent and headed back to her family. She walked past Joseph Ridges as he grabbed a crateful of blankets and clothing from his rescue wagon. As he did so, a raggedy doll tumbled out of a box crammed with goods. Harvey picked it up, and, dusting the snow off, he handed it to Emma.

"This must be for the little girl," Harvey said gesturing toward Suzannah.

Suzannah embraced the doll. Rescuers raced from one child to another distributing the soup and bread. Emma counted heads. Everyone was up except for James and Papa. The two were sound asleep. Emma carried two bowls of soup toward the men hoping the smell would awaken them.

"Papa. James, come get up. The bugle has called," she said.

There was no movement. Emma nudged James and nudged her father.

"Come on, help is here," she said.

Neither budged.

"Please, get up!" Emma cried as she nudged them.

Papa let out a soft groan.

"He's dead, Mary," Papa said.

"Papa!" Emma knelt next to the two men.

“Papa! James! Help is here, and there’s food, for Heaven’s sake, get up,” Emma pleaded.

“Come on now!”

“Mary,” Papa spoke softly. This time he was smiling.

Emma kissed James’ forehead and slowly covered his face with his torn blanket.

“Mary, don’t worry about the little ones,” Papa murmured. He reached across to Emma.

“There’s help here now. Papa, there’s food,” she cried.

She moistened Papa’s lips with some of the soup, hoping it would invigorate him. Papa tried eating but was too weak. He could only sip a little at a time.

Little Thom plowed through the snow to reach Emma. The rest of the Girdlestones quickly followed. They knelt down, encircling Papa and James.

“What’s wrong with Papa?” Little Thom asked. “Why won’t he get up? Is he frozen cold too?”

Papa continued to mutter as he talked about Great Melton. It was time to get the crops in. The fields were tilled. Grandpa Joseph was waiting for Papa, as were his uncles. He needed to hurry. The bugle had called.

“I’ve got to go…home. James, get…the horses. Father, Mary, I’m coming.”

Emma and her siblings turned to each other and stared. There was so much joy in their father’s voice. It was suddenly the same old Papa. He was happy. He was smiling. He sat up and reached forward.

“Papa. Please, don’t go,” Emma begged.

"The bugle has called," Papa murmured as he took his last breath.

Emma stopped crying; she was happy for him, that at last he was at peace with Mama. Yet the little ones cried, missing their papa.

CHAPTER THIRTEEN

Rescuers gathered the surviving company members; yet, sadly, there was one or two from every family who failed to make it through the night. Sounds of gratitude mixed with cries of sorrow pierced the air as pioneers realized how very lucky or how very unfortunate they had been during the night.

Joseph Ridges approached Franklin Richards.

"There shouldn't be any of them alive, President Richards," Joseph Ridges whispered to the Apostle as they headed to the mass grave. Richards nodded in agreement.

"A father and son by the name of Girdlestone; they helped dig this grave and buried the dead yesterday. They literally dug their own grave," Ridges said.

At the gravesite they found Captain Willie and John Chislett unearthing the hole dug the previous night. Emma stood nearby and her siblings gathered near her side.

Emma bit her lip and fought back the tears as she looked at the nine children who were now her responsibility. Suzannah and Thom clung to her skirts. The men gently removed dirt and brush from the grave.

"Why wouldn't Papa wake up?" Suzannah cried. "I keep a talkin' to him and givin' him hugs, but he won't get up and help me button my buttons," she complained.

"Papa is with Mama now, Suzannah. He can't help you, but I can," Emma said, bending down and fumbling with Suzy's buttons.

Joseph Ridges and Captain Willie lowered Papa and James into the ground. Once again there was no solemn reading of scripture or prayers sent heavenward.

"They gave the last of their strength," John Chislett said.

The Girdlestones watched as the men threw dirt over their family members. Benjamin, William, and John comforted the younger children.

"There, there, it's going to be all right," Benjamin said.

"Don't cry. Papa's with Mama now. So is James," John said.

A peace seemed to settle upon the children.

"It's the Welsh in ye," Emma could have sworn she heard her father say. Emma imagined her parents nearby with Papa telling his children to snap out of it. "Get going. You've been rescued. You can finish what your mother and I started," her father was saying.

"It's going to be all right," Emma said as she wrapped her arms around her siblings.

In the distance, Emma heard the bugle call.

CHAPTER FOURTEEN

Shortly after Papa and James were buried, Emma gathered her siblings around a campfire. Rescuers brought them warm food and blankets.

"Thank you for your kindness," Emma said to each who came to the family's aid.

Looking around the devastated campsite, Emma saw that other families had suffered a worse fate than hers. Many had frozen fingers and limbs. Captain Willie went around the campsite finding those with urgent needs. He was followed by men who provided medical care. Emma headed toward Captain Willie.

"Emma, is your family in need of any care?" Captain Willie asked.

"I believe they'll be fine. Is there anything that I can do to help?"

"My goodness, yes. Sister Emma, this is Brother Hanks, Ephraim Hanks. He has studied medicine," Captain Willie said as Emma extended her hand to Ephraim Hanks.

"Sister Emma, I need someone to bring me hot

water. I may need a knife," he said.

"I'll get the water," she said, and hurried back toward her campfire. She threw snow into all the kettles that would fit on the campfire.

"Frontier medicine," Emma said as she brought Ephraim kettles of hot water. Ephraim washed away the dead tissue of frostbite victims, then cleaned the wounds with Castile soap. Often the soap and water wasn't enough, and Ephraim Hanks had to remove frozen feet and hands with his sharp butcher knife.

After each surgery, Emma returned to the Girdlestone family campfire, where she washed and cleaned Ephraim's knives with boiling water. She held the knives over a flame to sterilize them.

"It has been cleansed by fire," Emma said.

While the surgery nauseated her, she handed each patient a piece of wood to bite down on as their limbs were removed. Emma gently wiped their foreheads during the process. When the snow turned scarlet, Emma turned away and closed her eyes.

Yet, each time Ephraim operated, that piece of wood proved unnecessary. No one, not once, ever seemed to be in pain. Emma marveled at Ephraim's skill and at the divine presence that comforted those who were so in need.

"Brother, are you all right?" Emma asked a fellow pioneer as he hobbled away on roughly made crutches.

"I felt nothing, Sister Emma. There was no pain," he said.

Not one of those requiring the amputations complained.

"Thank you, Brother Hanks. You saved my life," they said.

"My child was suffering so horribly. You relieved her of that," one mother said as she carried the child away.

"Brother Ephraim. You have saved many a limb and most assuredly many a life. You have blessed our company," Emma said when just a few travelers remained and needed only minor care.

"The Savior is the healer, not me. I think I can continue alone, Sister Emma, your family needs you."

Emma gathered her skirts and trudged to her family's campsite. She gathered up her family's possessions, including Mama's china dishes and her vases from the bottom of the handcart. Nestled beside them was Emma's handkerchief. She grabbed the treasures and kicked the old handcart's wheels.

"That's the end of you," she said. The craft toppled over as if to say that it could go no more. "The cart has given up the ghost as well."

Emma limped toward Joseph Ridges' wagon. Others abandoned their handcarts. The tiny worn out crafts lay strewn across the valley.

Margaret Dalglish insisted on keeping her handcart. Despite most of the rawhide being torn off the wheels and the wobbly craft falling apart, Margaret insisted on pulling it to Salt Lake.

"Sister Dalglish, we've got wagons," said Joseph Ridges. "You can ride with us. That handcart barely moves, and we still have seven hundred miles to go." He tried loosening Margaret's tight grip on her handcart. "Please, Sister, don't be foolish."

Margaret stood her ground. "Brother Ridges, I started with this handcart, and I will finish with this handcart."

Emma said, "Sister Margaret, please, I'll feel so very guilty riding in the wagon while you pull your cart."

"Sister Emma, it's my choice. Don't fret," Margaret said.

Too tired, cold, and hungry to argue, Emma and her family loaded Ridges' wagon.

Emma watched the camp disappear as Joseph Ridges' wagon took her and the surviving Girdlestone children away from the campsite and toward Salt Lake City. The gentle rocking motion of the wagon soon caused the children to fall asleep underneath a mountain of comforters.

Emma bid farewell to her parents and brother buried beneath the frozen trail. For a brief moment Emma saw James, Papa, and Mama waving goodbye from behind a clump of trees. Papa looked tall and strong, just like he had when they left Great Melton; Mama looked younger than Emma ever remembered; and James looked as healthy as a horse.

Emma blinked and they disappeared.

"How are you all back there?" Ridges asked from the driver's seat. "I know it's kind of crowded, but it's the best we could do. You folks caught us by surprise."

Ridges was handsome with dark brown eyes and pitch black hair—perhaps what Papa once looked like.

"We're fine. We're just so thankful you came when you did," Emma said. Emma looked out the front of the wagon while Ridges rambled about his great musical career in Salt Lake. "The man is handsome but talks too much," she thought.

The sun shone, and the snow sparkled against its bright rays. "Amazing how something that nearly killed us all now looks so heavenly," Emma mused.

She leaned back and closed her eyes while Ridges talked about an organ he was building. He said something about bringing it over from Australia, and how Brigham Young himself had commissioned the work.

"It took two teams of mules to get the pipes here to the valley," he said.

"My mother was a pianist," Emma blurted, breaking into Ridges' babble. "She played every day and we sang along with her. She wanted to bring the piano, but we only had the handcart."

"They all will play," Mama often told Papa, reminding him that Emma had a strong ear for music.

"She can play everything she hears. She must have lessons," Mama had said. Emma smiled at the memory.

"My mother insisted that I practice every day," she recalled.

"Maybe you'll get another piano in Salt Lake," he said. "Perhaps I could build you one."

"Mama had me take lessons," Emma said. "I was only six years old, but I thought the devil would surely get me if I didn't keep practicing. My teacher, Mrs. Gardner, promised me 'outer darkness and the weeping and gnashing of teeth.' if I didn't," Emma said. "I hated practicing, and I hated Mrs. Gardner. But it made Mama and Papa happy, so I played and practiced."

The wagon hit a bump that jostled the convoy, causing Suzannah to whimper.

"Mama!" she cried out and then fell back to sleep.

"It's a kind of rocky along this trail, but it won't be long till we reach Salt Lake," Ridges said.

"Thank Heavens," Emma sighed as she drifted into a deep warm slumber.

CHAPTER FIFTEEN

Emma woke up when Joseph Ridges called to her from the front of the wagon.

"We're at Emigration Canyon—not far from Salt Lake. You've made it to Zion! This is the place!" Ridges said.

Emma looked west toward the snow-covered mountains. As the wagons passed through Emigration Canyon, Margaret Dalglish finally stopped pulling her handcart. Emma watched the tiny woman give the cart one shove over the side of the mountain. She stood with her hands on her hips, watching it crash against rocks, throwing all of her worldly possessions down the mountainside.

Margaret waved goodbye to the handcart as it landed in pieces at the bottom of the canyon. She brushed her hands. "Good riddance to you and the devil. That's the end of the both of you!"

Joseph Ridges stopped his wagon. "Ready to ride now?" he asked.

"More than anything," Margaret answered. She climbed into the wagon, stepping over the

Girdlestone family.

"Margaret, what were you thinking? Everything you owned was in that handcart!" Emma said.

Margaret just shrugged. "I know. I don't care. I don't give a damn!" she said curling under a blanket next to Emma.

"It's not long for Salt Lake," Joseph promised.

When the rescue wagons stopped at the Endowment House, hundreds of Salt Lake residents rushed into the streets to help. Brigham Young helped the travelers out of their wagons.

"Sister, take my hand," Young urged Emma.

"Thank you, Brother," Emma said as she took in her new surroundings. She had no idea that the man who just helped her was the Prophet.

"Brother Young. Brigham Young," he said.

Emma froze.

"Brigham Young. The prophet!" she gasped. Emma steadied herself. "President Young, I, uh thank you. I, uh I'm honored to meet you. I do apologize I am so honored," she said, struggling for something appropriate to say.

"Sister, it is I who should be honored," Young said as he embraced Emma. "I'm so thankful you've finally made it here to the promised land. We have a home waiting for you."

"Thank you! I have all these brothers and sisters with me. Our parents passed away," she said.

One by one, Brigham Young helped the Girdlestone children from Ridges' wagon. Out came Jane, Suzannah, and Little Thomas. The Prophet held their hands and guided them into two wagons. Ben, John,

William, Robert, Elizabeth, and Sarah soon followed and climbed into the wagon. They bounced along the snowy Salt Lake City streets. They watched residents going in and out of stores. They came out of the shops with goods and produce piled high.

Earlier that summer a group of California men had stumbled across the Willie Company. They talked about the prosperity to be found in God's Country.

"The Mormon Valley, it's first rate," one gentleman said.

"The soil couldn't be more rich—dark and fertile," said another.

It was wonderful news to the travelers, and especially so for the Girdlestones, who were set on farming in Zion.

"We have so looked forward to reaching the Valley," Papa had said.

"It's wonderful to get such a good report. We've often wondered about growing anything in that desert," Willie told the men as they ate around the campfire.

"We couldn't believe it either, but everything grows in the Valley. The wheat and barley fields and the hay—it's all growing. The Mormons can get anything to grow," the men said. "In the middle of all that desert and sagebrush."

Papa and James wouldn't be able to fulfill that dream of planting their own crops in Zion's soil. Hopefully John, William, and Benjamin would carry out the family's dream.

The Girdlestones' wagon pulled up to their

temporary lodging with their British friends Priscilla and Elijah Girling.

Emma had known Priscilla since they lived in Norfolk. She had grown up with Priscilla and had been baptized with her on the very same day. Priscilla's parents, devout Ranting Methodists, had given her the boot for joining those "mad Mormons."

Emma had invited Priscilla to live with her family. She lived with the Girdlestones until she married Elijah Girling. The newlyweds headed to Zion shortly after.

Emma and Priscilla had kept in touch through letters that told all about Zion.

Arriving at the Girlings' home, Emma climbed out of the wagon and flew into the open arms of Priscilla and Elijah. Where Emma had once sheltered Priscilla, Priscilla now offered shelter to Emma and her family.

"Oh, Emma, you poor dear. How did you survive?" Priscilla cried.

All nine of Emma's brothers and sisters slowly made their way into the Girlings' spacious home.

"We heard in conference what happened. We knew you were coming with the Willie Handcart Company. We told President Young to bring you here," Priscilla said.

She guided Emma and her siblings up the stairs. "There's plenty of room, but the younger children will need to share the beds. We don't have quite enough."

"This is wonderful, Priscilla. It's Heaven on earth," Emma said.

"Just put some meat on those skinny bones of yours. Simply too thin, my dear Emma. We'll have to fatten you up!"

Elijah went up and down the stairs, bringing pitchers of warm water to the family. The steam rose from the water jugs as he placed them on a dresser.

The family hadn't bathed in weeks, and Emma hadn't realized how dirty they had become on the trail. She dipped a hand towel into the steamy water and washed her face with soap. Suds poured down her face and the streaks showed how filthy she had become.

The bar of soap reminded Emma of how they had used soap to grease the axles of the handcart after they ran out of grease.

During the summer the handcart's wheels would become so caked with dirt and sand that it wouldn't budge. First they greased the axle with leftover grease from breakfast. Papa and James poured water over the axles to get rid of the dirt, then the girls wiped them clean with their skirts. After the cleaning, they slathered the axles with more breakfast grease. The grease helped for several miles, but when that wore off, they relied on soap to oil their axles.

Emma dipped her hand towel into the wash bin; the water turned black. "Black as Papa's plowed Norfolk fields," she marveled.

She grabbed a pitcher of water and poured it over her dirty matted hair. She scrubbed her long tresses, and, as her hair dried, she was convinced it had changed color. Such was the case for Suzannah, whose blonde hair had become so dirty it looked brown. Emma helped her younger sister, scrubbing the little girl's hair.

"Emma, my hair, it's not brown like yours anymore!" Suzannah gasped.

"Not to worry. My hair was blonde when I was little, too. It will change and be just like mine and Mama's," Emma assured her.

Priscilla knocked on Emma's door.

"Is everyone respectable?" Priscilla asked as she peeked through the door. Emma opened the door to find Priscilla buried under a mountain of clean clothes and shoes.

"The sister's Relief Society helped gather these," she said.

"Oh, so pretty," Elizabeth and Sarah gushed as they grabbed dresses and held them up.

They were so overjoyed at getting the new clothing they thought nothing of privacy, and undressed quickly to try on the new garments. The sisters paraded around the room as they tossed their old worn out and filthy dresses onto the floor. When the dresses hit the floor, dust billowed from the worn out clothing.

Having had very little privacy while on the trail, Emma craved some solitude and moved into an adjoining room, where she tore off her once favorite blue muslin dress. Emma tried on the new yellow garment. It hung from her slender frame.

Emma slipped off what was left of her shoes. "My rags," she joked, recalling the last few weeks of tying her footwear to keep it together.

During the journey, Emma's shoes had become

threadbare. She had torn her petticoats and part of her skirts to tie the soles of her shoes together. Now she had a pair of clean wool socks and sturdy new shoes. Emma inspected her new shoes, amazed that they weren't covered with muck. She joined her sisters, where she added her old clothing to the pile. She kept her dark blue cape because it had belonged to Mama and tucked it inside a dresser drawer.

"Maybe we could burn these," Emma said as she inspected the pile of old soiled clothes.

"Now that's the Emma I remember," Priscilla said. "You look wonderful. A bit thin, but still lovely." She headed for the boys' room, where they could be heard splashing water and joking.

"We could make a mud pie!" joked Benjamin.

"It would taste better than all that rawhide soup Emma made," William chuckled.

Priscilla knocked on the door and handed the boys their new clothing that came with a pair of new suspenders. "Just in case they're too big. You all are a bit thin, to say the least."

"Look, no holes in the knees," Little Thomas said as he examined his new pants.

Shortly after, Priscilla called the Girdlestones to dinner.

"It's your first sit-down meal in God's Country!" said Elijah.

"This food is so pretty," Suzannah said.

Mountains of food were passed around the table. Suzannah grabbed a plate of roast beef and placed some on her plate.

Emma looked around the table at her brothers

and sisters grabbing platefuls food. William passed food to Benjamin, who took his time selecting his portion before handing the dish to John. Robert grabbed the plate from John, and Elizabeth yanked it out of his hands. Little Thom piled potatoes on his plate and covered them with a river of gravy.

Emma wrapped a piece of roast beef around her fork. She had never tasted such a delicious meal. The food did indeed taste wonderful here in Zion, the land of milk and honey.

***

ABOUT THE AUTHOR

Lisa Dayley graduated from the Metropolitan State College of Denver with a bachelor's degree in Mass Communications and Creative Writing. An award-winning writer and photographer, she has written for both newspapers and magazines. Dayley lives in Burley, Idaho with her husband Darrell. They have three children and one grandson.

www.ingramcontent.com/pod-product-compliance
Lightning Source LLC
LaVergne TN
LVHW091010080826
845145LV00003B/1208

9780979607042